DEADLY TRAP

ALSO BY HUGH PENTECOST

Julian Quist Mystery Novels:

THE STEEL PALACE
DIE AFTER DARK
HONEYMOON WITH DEATH
THE JUDAS FREAK
THE BEAUTIFUL DEAD
THE CHAMPAGNE KILLER
DON'T DROP TOMORROW

Pierre Chambrum Mystery Novels:

DEATH AFTER BREAKFAST
THE FOURTEEN DILEMMA
TIME OF TERROR
BARGAIN WITH DEATH
WALKING DEAD MAN
BIRTHDAY, DEATHDAY
THE DEADLY JOKE
GIRL WATCHER'S FUNERAL
THE GILDED NIGHTMARE
THE GOLDEN TRAP
THE EVIL MEN DO
THE SHAPE OF FEAR
THE CANNIBAL WHO OVERATE

A David Cotter Mystery Novel:

MURDER AS USUAL

Hugh Pentecost

DEADLY TRAP

A Red Badge Novel of Suspense

DODD, MEAD & COMPANY
NEW YORK

Printed in the United States of America

1 2 3 4 5 6 7 8 9 10

Library of Congress Cataloging in Publication Data

Philips, Judson Pentecost, date
Deadly trap.

(A Red badge novel of suspense)
I. Title.
PZ3.P5412DAW [PS3531.H442] 813'.5'2 78-14530
ISBN 0-396-07606-8

PART ONE

CHAPTER ONE

It was absurd, but the quiet of the place was a little more than Lydia Morton could take. Julian had proposed the holiday, a week at Pat Altman's camp on Lake Toromog in the Berkshires. Altman was in Europe, the place was theirs. They hadn't had a holiday since God knows when. The opportunity might not come again for a long, long time. The activities of Julian Quist Associates, public relations experts, located in a steel-and-glass finger pointing to the sky over Grand Central Station in New York City, seldom stopped spinning in high gear.

"We can't afford to take the time," Lydia had said, sensing somehow that it wasn't quite what she wanted. The best restaurants in town, the theater, the ballet, the symphony, Quist's deluxe apartment overlooking the East River, and the exciting pressures of selling glamorous and famous people to the world—those things were Lydia's life. Those things and looking beautiful as a high-fashion model for the clients and for Julian, who was her man. A rustic camp in the woods promised to be a little too far removed from all the things that made Lydia's life tick.

Neither could Lydia visualize Julian in the woods! Julian,

tall, elegant, his golden hair worn long but carefully styled, whose closets in the Beekman Place apartment contained more suits, expertly tailored, than Lydia had ever been able to count. Julian represented the epitome of sophisticated city living.

Among the things they could do at Altman's camp, Julian had suggested, were swimming, fishing, sailing, hiking—

"I could never bait a fishhook," Lydia said.

"I will bait your fishhook, luv," Julian said.

Somehow she couldn't imagine his slender, expressive hands messing around with worms. Not that there was anything effete, for all his mod style, about Julian. Lydia had lived with him for some years now and she had reason to know how very male he was. But out in the woods? Hiking?

The camp was something of a surprise when they got to it one late afternoon. The setting, on the edge of a lake, with wooded hills all around, was as imagined. The exterior of the log-cabin-type building was as imagined. Even the caretaker, one Joe Wellman, was in character—tall, broad-shouldered, scraggly beard, Levi's, and a blue-and-red-checked work shirt. Joe opened the cabin for them, and it was not what they'd expected.

"But we should have," Quist said later.

Pat Altman, millionaire real-estate operator, hadn't sacrificed an ounce of physical comfort and luxury in his "camp." Joe Wellman explained that it had its own electric generator, air conditioning if it got a little too hot at midday, baseboard electric heat to augment the huge fieldstone fireplace if the nights grew chill. There was an ice-making machine behind the bar, a washing machine and dryer, a dishwasher, and a garbage-disposal unit in the kitchen. If anything, it was more sophisticated in its equipment than Quist's Beekman Place apartment. Wellman turned over the keys to the boathouse, showed them where Altman kept his expensive fishing tackle, explained the workings of a color TV set and a hi-fi system, and left them to "rough it."

They unpacked the simple camping clothes they'd brought with them, admired the king-size bed in the sleeping quarters, made themselves a perfect dry martini, and went outdoors to breathe the air—fresh, unpolluted, marvelous air. Lydia made a simple supper and they sat in front of the fire, listening to the peepers.

Quist glanced at his watch. "I don't think I've been to bed as early as nine o'clock since I was four years old, but, so help me, luv, I can't keep my eyes open any longer."

They slept in the giant bed, touching gently.

It was a curious experience, Quist suggested over breakfast: "Like letting the air out of a balloon." All the tension of their regular high-pressure kind of living oozed away and left them with no energy for anything but total relaxation. They should try the boat, they should swim, they should hike. They just lolled in the sun, and snoozed, and laughed at themselves. "Some campers!"

The afternoon of the second day, Quist announced that he was going to "risk" taking a walk in the woods. Lydia declined an invitation to join him. She hadn't the energy to get up out of the deck chair in which she was stretched out under a huge pine tree facing the lake.

It was three o'clock in the afternoon when Quist took off.

At four o'clock Lydia was surprised by the length of his walk. At five o'clock she was angry with him for having left her alone for so long. At six o'clock she was genuinely concerned. She was suddenly conscious of the one missing luxury at the camp. No telephone.

They had stopped at Joe Wellman's cottage about two miles down the wooded road on their way in. Lydia decided to drive the Mercedes down there and realized, when she got to the car, that the keys were in Quist's pocket.

She walked—jogging at intervals. It took her a little better than twenty minutes to get to Wellman's place. Wellman was out in his backyard splitting some kindling with a sharp-blade hatchet.

"Something wrong, Miss Morton?" he asked.

She told him. Quist had been gone now for more than three hours. He must be lost, or he'd had some kind of accident.

"Out in the boat?" Wellman asked.

"No. He walked up into the woods."

"Pretty hard to get lost up there," Wellman said. "Looks like wild country from the camp, but there are actually dozens of cabins up in the woods, most all of them occupied this time of year. Maybe he ran into friends and lost track of time."

"We don't have any friends up here," Lydia said.

"I'll drive you back and take a look," Wellman said. "He'll probably be there."

Quist wasn't there. Wellman, apparently unconcerned, walked off into the woods, leaving Lydia at the camp in case Quist appeared from another direction. It was after seven when Wellman returned. He looked a little worried now.

"No sign of him," he said. "I inquired at a couple of camps on the ridge. No one's seen him." He lifted his head to look up into the sky. A helicopter was passing over them. "Too bad we can't get word to him. He might spot Mr. Quist if he knew to look."

"How much more daylight?" Lydia asked, practically.

"Daylight saving—about eight-thirty it turns dark," Wellman said.

A little more than an hour of light.

"Shouldn't we—perhaps—be getting help, Mr. Wellman?" Lydia asked.

Wellman was still watching the helicopter, which now

disappeared over the line of trees.

"Aren't any steep cliffs or abandoned quarries up in those woods," he said. "No risky areas. But I suppose a guy could sprain, or even break, his ankle in a bathtub. Thing is, if he yelled long enough he'd almost certainly be heard. Lot of cottages, people moseying around outdoors." Wellman focused on Lydia. "How about Mr. Quist's condition?"

"Condition?"

"His health. Heart okay? Stuff like that."

"He's fine. Regular checkups. He had one just recently."

"Well, you sit tight," Wellman said. "I'll drive back down to my place and phone the state police. What we need is a little manpower."

"You have a phone?"

"Last one on the line," Wellman said. "No poles beyond my place." Somehow she hated to have him go, hated to be left alone. "Is there any way to start Julian's car without the keys?" she asked.

"I suppose a mechanic could do it for you," Wellman said. "Is it locked?"

"Only the ignition."

"Maybe I can get her working for you when I get back," Wellman said. He took off in his jeep for the telephone and help.

Lydia sat down on a large flat stone outside the cabin. Her legs felt a little rubbery under her. Julian had been gone for almost five hours now. He would never in this world have left her in suspense like this voluntarily. She strained to hear something. Then her heart pounded against her ribs. Someone was coming through the woods from up above the cabin. Lydia stood up, Julian's name on her lips.

But it wasn't Julian. A small boy, maybe twelve or thirteen Lydia guessed, came into the clearing and headed straight for her.

"You the lady whose husband is missing?" the boy asked.

She didn't correct the "husband" part of his question. This was not the moment to explain that she and Julian had never married because their relationship was so good as it was they hadn't wanted to risk anything that might change it. She just nodded to the boy.

"I'm Jerry Tinker," the boy said. "My folks have a camp just up over the ridge. Joe Wellman told us about your husband. I've been looking around. No sign of him so far. You friends of Mr. Altman's?"

"He loaned us the camp for a week," Lydia said.

"That's right. He's in Europe, isn't he? Your husband have a gun, ma'am?"

"No."

"There was some shooting up in the woods earlier," the boy said. "Sometime—oh, around three-thirty, I guess. I heard it and I wondered about it. Single shot. All this property is posted. No hunting. Too many cabins and people hidden away. I thought maybe your husband didn't know that and took a potshot at something—a bird, or a rabbit or something."

"He doesn't have a gun," Lydia said, and felt a dampness in the palms of her hands. "No interest in hunting."

The boy frowned with a kind of intense seriousness. "Someone fooling around with a gun," he said. "There could have been—an accident."

"Oh my God!" Lydia said.

"Joe still looking?" the boy asked.

"He's gone for the state police," Lydia said.

"Good. They'll have torches. We won't be able to see much in another half hour. You better tell the troopers I heard a gunshot, Mrs.—?"

"Ms. Morton," Lydia said.

The boy looked puzzled. "I thought Joe Wellman said

your husband's name was Quist."

"It is."

"Oh."

"In our business I keep my maiden name."

"Oh. Well, I didn't mean to scare you, Miss Morton. The gunshot may have had nothing to do with what's happened to him. Just a coincidence."

"Let's hope so."

"I'll keep looking while it's still light," the boy said, and trotted off.

Lydia was alone again in the approaching darkness.

Wellman's jeep, headlights on, came up the trail. He reported the state police were sending help. Lydia told him about Jerry Tinker and the gunshot. Wellman looked concerned.

"Mr. Quist didn't have a gun?"

"No."

"Some crazy bastard sees something moving in the bushes and takes a shot at it. Have to be a stranger, you'd think, who didn't know the rules around here."

"You think—?"

"I don't think anything yet, Miss Morton. I was home all afternoon. Didn't hear any gunshot. Sound carries and echoes up here. But I had my power saw going about that time—three-thirty. You didn't hear it?"

"I went to sleep after Julian left," she said.

The police car arrived a few minutes later. It was suddenly dark. Wellman introduced Sergeant Stryker and Trooper Fisher. In the light from the car they looked military, efficient. Wellman told them the Tinker boy's story of the gunshot. They were all obviously thinking the same thing. Quist had been put out of business by a stray bullet.

"Three-thirty," Stryker said. "You say Quist left here about three, Miss Morton?"

She nodded.

"He couldn't have gone too far in half an hour," Stryker said. "Not headed for any place in particular?"

"I expected him back in half an hour," Lydia said. "He just went for a stroll."

"We'll do what we can," Stryker said. "But it's going to be difficult until morning and daylight."

"If he's wounded that may be too late!" Lydia said.

"I know, ma'am. We'll do our best."

The troopers took off into the woods, bright torchlights sweeping the darkness ahead of them.

"I wonder if I might use your phone, Mr. Wellman, to call the city?" Lydia asked.

"Sure. Drive you down," Wellman said.

None of the help seemed real, the troopers, Wellman, the boy. Strangers, thinking their thoughts behind strange, cautious faces. Lydia felt a desperate need for someone friendly and familiar. Julian Quist Associates consisted of four people at the top: Quist at the very top, the boss; Lydia, in charge of research and development; Dan Garvey, a former professional football player, who handled all the various promotions in the world of sports; and Bobby Hilliard, a young Jimmy Stewart, whose special talent was dealing with temperamental and egocentric clients.

Dan Garvey, Quist's closest friend, was the person Lydia needed in this time of anxiety. At this time of night Dan was probably out on the town somewhere, dining with some delightful and likely lady. He sounded impatient when he answered the phone. As a matter of fact, he had been at his front door when the phone rang, headed for a rendezvous with just such a lady.

"Lydia! Country life getting you, doll?"

She told him what had happened. Quist had now been missing more than six hours. There was the gunshot; there were the obvious conclusions drawn by the troopers, by Wellman, and by Jerry Tinker.

Garvey's voice turned hard and practical. "Take me half an hour to change out of my dinner jacket and get my car out of the garage," he said.

"Two hours and a half to drive up here," Lydia said, tears near the surface.

"Two hours if I don't get pinched," Garvey said. "Sit tight, doll."

"I wish to God people would stop telling me to sit tight!" she shouted into a suddenly dead telephone.

CHAPTER TWO

Julian Quist wasn't a woodsman or a botanist. He was strictly a city man, had been all his life. But he was in first-class physical condition. Three days a week he played squash, vigorously and violently, at the Athletic Club. He lifted weights on the terrace of his apartment. Occasionally he boxed with Dan Garvey, who had been an intercollegiate boxing champion before he turned to professional football, and Garvey had his hands full with Quist. The uphill climb through the woods imposed no strain on well-conditioned legs. He breathed deeply because it gave him pleasure to take in the unaccustomed clean air.

He told himself, as he paused at a high point to look down at the lake, that while the woods were beautiful, while the little boat that skimmed the lake, its red sail filled by the breeze, was picture-post-card perfect, it all wasn't really his thing. Forty-eight hours and he already missed the city, the taxi noises, the jackhammers tearing up the streets endlessly; missed the excitement of his business, which brought him into daily contact with politicians and movie stars, with big corporations that owned half the world, with book publishers and theatrical producers, with charities sponsored by the spotlighted people of high society, and with the promoters of the world's greatest sporting events. He missed all these forces, which kept him in perpetual motion. He missed his office, with its modern furniture and its modern paintings; he missed the people who were part of his daily life—Dan Garvey; and his incredible secretary, Connie Parmalee, who anticipated his every need, often instinctively ahead of Lydia in that department; Bobby Hilliard, who never lost his cool with difficult people; and the glamorous Gloria Chard, who sat at a circular desk in the outer office and protected him from idiots. He missed them all and wished they could be here. What he really wished, he told himself with a wry smile, was that he was back there with them. He wondered what would happen if he went down the hill and suggested to Lydia that they pack up and go back to where it all was. He had persuaded her to come, somewhat against her will. Now he'd have to tell her she'd been right. Camping out, even in Pat Altman's supercivilized log cabin, was not for them.

He turned to go back down the hill, having been away not more than twenty minutes, when he heard it. It sounded like someone crying, bitterly, only a few yards away from him on the up side of the hill.

He called out. "You got trouble? Can I help?"

The crying instantly stopped, followed by the sound of something being dragged, or dragging itself, through the brush—away from him.

Quist tried again. "Can I help you?"

He moved toward the sound of dragging, and it seemed to

accelerate. He parted the low-hanging branches of some sort of evergreen and saw what it was. Saw, and was shocked by a kind of savage snarling a few feet away. A dog, some kind of water spaniel Quist guessed, his coat matted, faced the man. The animal's eyes were bloodshot, with a wild look in them. Blood and foam flecked the lips, which were drawn back from white teeth and that warning snarl. The dog moved away, awkwardly, painfully, and the dragging sound was reproduced. It was caused by an iron trap, its teeth clamped viciously over the dog's right hind leg. That leg was mangled and bloody. The dog had obviously been trying to chew himself free. Its foot and the tendons and bones above the steel teeth were almost eaten through.

"Easy, boy," Quist said, and stepped closer.

The dog went into a frenzy of snarls and growls, sheer terror in every move and sound. It moved away, little cries of pain punctuating the warnings. Quist knew that if he could reach the animal he could set it free from its torture. The dog was equally determined to die defending himself.

Just ahead Quist saw a patch of bright sunlight, some sort of clearing. The dog reached it and turned to face his pursuer. His bloodied tongue hung out of his mouth as he gasped for breath.

"Easy, boy. If you'll just let me at it—"

The dog twisted his body, in agony, in the opposite direction. He had heard something that Quist hadn't.

"Son of a bitch!" a man's voice said. It was a cold, angry voice.

Quist turned his head and saw that this sunlit clearing was just outside another camp cabin. A man was standing on a flat stone doorstep. He was a tall, dark, slender man. Black glasses in wire frames shielded his eyes from the sun. He was wearing a blue, pin-striped, vested suit, white shirt, silk-figured tie. These were not the clothes for the woods. He was right out of some custom-tailoring establishment.

The man looked down at the agonized dog, reached inside his jacket and produces a bulky-looking handgun. He brought it down in a slow arc and, quite literally, blew the dog's head off.

"For God's sake!" Quist said, in shock. "I could have set him free!"

The man's elbow was bent now, the gun pointing toward the sky. "Put him out of his misery," the man said, "and let you know for sure this isn't a toy. It's loaded you now know."

It was a big gun, a .44, Quist guessed. He knew weapons. And this man knew how to use it. That one shot had caught the suffering dog right between the eyes and blown its skull apart.

The door behind the man opened and another man appeared, white haired, tanned face. He was also city dressed.

"What the hell?" he said.

"Visitor," the man with the black glasses said. "Damned dog attracted attention."

"And a gunshot?" the white-haired man said. "Better get him inside."

"You heard," the man with the black glasses said to Quist. His arm lowered and the gun pointed straight at Quist's heart.

"What is this?" Quist said, standing very still.

"You came to the wrong party, buster," the man said. "Walk into the cabin, unless you'd like to be prompted a little more painfully."

There wasn't the slightest doubt that the man meant what he said. Quist moved, his legs feeling suddenly stiff and awkward. He walked past the dead dog, past the man—who turned in a slow circle, keeping the gun straight on target—and into the cabin.

This was far less elaborate than Pat Altman's place. Rustic, hand-carpentered furniture. Paintings on the wall suggested that the owner might be an artist of sorts. They were crude primitives. A hobby, not a profession, Quist thought. The white-haired man was standing by a picture window that overlooked the lake.

"He seem to be alone?" he asked.

The door closed behind Quist and the man with the black glasses answered. "No sign of anyone else."

"Damned gunshot," the white-haired man said.

He wasn't the only person in the room. Sitting huddled in the corner of a sort of bench couch was a woman. She was a dark, rather sensational-looking girl in her early twenties. Wide black eyes looked almost pleadingly at Quist.

"Who are you?" the white-haired man asked Quist.

"You first," Quist said. "Who are you?"

"It doesn't matter," the man said.

"You've got a name, haven't you?"

The man shrugged. "Smith—Jones—Brown, take your pick. Yours?"

"Quist. Julian Quist."

"Camping here somewhere?"

"Cabin about a mile down the hill. It belongs to a friend. He loaned it to me."

"Alone?"

Quist thought of Lydia and said, "Alone."

"He's lying, of course," the man with the black glasses said.

"Of course," the other man said.

Quist turned to the man with the black glasses. "You got a name."

A thin smile moved the man's lips. "He's Smith, I'm Jones," he said.

"We're going to have to get out of here," the man named

"Smith" said. "I'll get in touch with Dixon on the CB."

"People will come looking for this character after a while," Jones said. "I could find a place to dump him."

"That won't stop them looking for him," Smith said. "What do you do for a living, Quist?"

"Public relations," Quist said. It was better to answer questions while he tried to figure out some move.

"For God sake," Jones said. "Julian Quist Associates! They sell movie stars, athletes, the moon, if someone wants to buy it. Big noise."

"Bad luck," Smith said. He turned to Quist. "You're forcing us to make a rather hurried move, Mr. Quist. Bad luck for us and for you. You've walked into a kidnapping, big-time stuff. The lady is our hostage. There's money and political power involved. So much money and so much power that it can't be allowed to fail because of a damn-fool dog—and you."

Quist looked at the girl. There was a blank look on her face, as though she didn't understand what was being said, or was in shock.

"When you don't return to your camp they'll come looking for you," Smith said. "It won't do us any good just to get rid of you. They'll come here eventually, whether you're here or not. From what Jarvis says you may have some value to us alive."

"Jarvis?" Quist asked.

The man with the black glasses grinned. "Jarvis-Jones," he said.

"You can make it easy for yourself, or you can make it hard," Smith said to Quist. He turned to Jarvis. "You'd better keep watch outside. Better fasten him to that chair."

Jarvis went to a raincoat that was hanging on a hook near the door. From a pocket he produced an ordinary pair of police handcuffs. He snapped one end over Quist's right wrist and the other to the arm of a heavy wooden armchair. He was trapped, Quist thought, just as the unfortunate dog had been.

Jarvis, his gun slipped back into its holster under his jacket, went out the front door. Smith disappeared into a rear room, out of sight and sound. Quist was alone with the girl.

"You seem to be all in one piece," he said.

The girl gave him a blank look.

"You care to tell me who you are and what they're asking for you?"

The girl leaned forward. Words poured out of her in a language Quist didn't recognize.

"You don't speak English?" he asked.

Another flood of words in the same unintelligible language.

Quist could speak French rather fluently and tried her with that. No recognition form the girl.

He tried some childish sign language, pointing to himself, and saying "Julian" and then pointing at her. "Me Tarzan, you Jane." No result. But after several tries he thought she said "Tina" or "Tiana." Tiana seemed more likely, somehow, and he repeated it. Finally she nodded and leaned back on the couch, exhausted.

Tiana. He'd never heard that name. It didn't tie in with any culture he knew. Big money, big politics, Smith had said. He managed to extricate one of the thin little black cigars he smoked from his breast pocket with his free hand. His lighter was in the pocket on the awkward side and he had to go through contortions to get it. It was an engraved gold Dunhill Lydia had given him for his last birthday. He got the cigar going and pocketed the lighter on his free side.

How long would it be, he wondered, before Lydia would become concerned about him and get help?

Smith came out of the back room. The white-haired man looked worried.

"You'd better do a little praying, Quist, that your friends don't get worried too soon," he said. "We're moving out of here by helicopter, but it will be two, three hours before our man can make it. If your people come looking for you before that, you and they—" He shrugged, and went to the front door to look for Jarvis. "All clear?" he called out.

"So far," Jarvis called back. "Maybe his friends don't love him."

"Don't count on it," Smith said, and closed the door.

"You own this cabin?" Quist asked.

"No, but don't hope the owner will show up. He's a pop singer who's doing a week in Philadelphia."

Lydia might not go for serious help soon enough, Quist thought. The owner of the cabin wouldn't show. But would anyone come looking for the unhappy dog that lay dead out in the yard? Jarvis probably would have moved the body out of sight, but would that prevent an anxious owner from coming to look?

CHAPTER THREE

Dan Garvey was a man born to express himself in physical terms. Sports had been his life since Little League baseball days. He had been a star baseball and football player in high school, had won a football scholarship to a Big Ten college, where he had made All-American and been an intercollegiate light-heavyweight boxing champion on the side. After college he had gone into professional football, where sports writers rated him with Gale Sayers and O. J. Simpson among the all-time great running backs. After four years he was one of the highest-paid players, was making a small fortune on TV commercials, and appeared to be set for life. Then, one late fall afternoon, trying to cut back on a slippery field, something popped in his right knee and that was that. Other players had suffered the same kind of injury, gone under the knife, and come back almost as good as new.

Garvey couldn't take the "almost." He could never make his moves without thinking, without wondering. What once had been instinctive now had to be planned. It cost him a step and was the difference between being *the* man and just a run-of-the-mill back. That wasn't for him. But what was for him?

He was offered jobs by admirers. He could sell life insurance. He could work in a brokerage house. He could do the color commentary on TV—and he did for a season. He hated it. He hated watching, not being a part of it. After that one season he began to drift. He had money in the bank. He began to drink more than was good for him. He chased after women, successfully because of his dark good looks and enormous vitality. He also began to make a nuisance of himself in public places. One night in Willard's Backyard, a famous East Side bar and nightclub, his eye caught a rather breathtaking redhead and he moved in, brushing aside an elderly banker type who was the girl's escort. The banker type demanded help from the management. Willard, the smooth proprietor, tried reason and was pushed aside. Then Garvey found himself confronted by a tall blond dude wearing, for God's sake, a pink dinner jacket.

"You better cool it, Dan," the blond dude said.

Garvey measured him. He could take this character, he thought, with one arm tied behind him. He started a leisurely swing from left field and found himself caught in an agonizing armlock. The blond dude had been a lot more competent than Garvey had expected.

"Let's go talk somewhere," the blond dude said.

Rather than make a fool of himself trying to struggle out of an unbreakable hold, Garvey let himself be lead into Willard's private office. Alone there, the blond dude released his hold.

"Now, if you want to have at me in private—" the blond said.

Garvey rubbed his aching arm. "Do I know you?" he asked.

"Julian Quist," the blond said.

"It goes with the territory, I guess," Garvey said.

"What I've been wanting to talk to you about was a job," Quist said.

Garvey's smile soured. "Charity case?" he asked. "I'm not broke—yet, Quist."

"You're wasting your talents," Quist said.

"My one talent was to cut inside tackle and run through the secondary," Garvey said. "No more."

"You have a love for sports," Quist said. "You have a name that makes people listen to you. You've got energy you haven't got any place to put. I've got a job where all that can be used."

"Goddamn it, man, you don't have to feel sorry for me!"

"I don't, I can use you," Quist said.

Quist had contracted to promote a big new sports arena on the Island. There would be basketball, and hockey, and fights, and track meets, and horse shows, and the circus, and a hatful of special events.

"All of this is going to need goosing, and promoting, and overseeing. It's got to be class managed. I have an idea you're the man for it."

"You don't know me," Garvey said.

"I've played hunches all my life," Quist said. He mentioned a salary, plus bonuses and commissions.

Garvey's eyes widened. "You're kidding!"

Quist took a wallet out of his pocket and produced a business card. "Come to see me at ten tomorrow morning and we'll close the deal," he said. "I suggest you go somewhere now and sleep it off. After tomorrow you won't have time to shoot up saloons."

That was the beginning for Garvey. He was fascinated by Quist's elaborate office the next morning, by the glamorous receptionist, by the efficient secretary with the copper-red hair and the faintly tinted granny glasses, who took him to Quist's private office—with its chromium-trimmed bar on wheels, its modern furniture, which looked uncomfortable and yet fitted around you like a lover's arms—where he met Quist's "associates." They were Lydia Morton and Bobby Hilliard. He took one look at Lydia and told himself, "That's for me!" He found out a little later that she was not for him and never would be for him. She belonged to Quist.

Quist, in his pale-blue linen suit, and what Garvey thought was a foppish manner, was an unknown quantity. Not my type, Garvey thought, but he remembered the armlock that had quieted him in Willard's Backyard.

Now, after some years, Quist was his best, his most cherished friend. Garvey had become an "associate," sharing in the firm's profits. He and Quist argued and battled over policies and Quist always won, because he had the deciding vote even if the count was three to one against him. The result was respect. Quist was almost always right.

Garvey taught himself to forget about Lydia. They worked together, she doing research and writing brilliant press releases for his project, the sports arena. She treated him like a dear friend, a beloved brother. Just once, when they had been working together for hours on some promotion, he had suggested to her that a man and a woman couldn't spend that kind of time together without something more. She had said she was pleased he felt that way about her, flattered, but unfortunately she was totally committed. "It would be fun," she'd said, "but too much else matters."

Now she needed him.

Twenty miles north of the city, on the Saw Mill River Parkway, a cop stopped him. He'd been driving eighty miles an hour in a fifty-five-mile-an-hour speed zone. The stone-faced trooper looked at his license.

"You Dan Garvey, the football player?" he asked.

"Used to be," Garvey said.

"You know how fast you were going, Dan?"

Garvey explained to him about his friend Quist. That there might have been a shooting accident. That he had to get to Lake Toromog "yesterday."

The trooper handed back his license. "Follow me to the end of the parkway," he said.

It was a wild fifty miles, driven at a speed Garvey could scarcely believe. At the end of the ride, the trooper, grinning at Garvey's tense white face, gave him a shortcut direction to the lake. He arrived at Pat Altman's cabin half an hour earlier than he'd believe possible.

Lydia greeted him at the door. She was suddenly in his arms, crying softly. The local troopers had found no sign of Quist. Joe Wellman had gone into town to round up some local volunteers. They weren't going to give up the hunt, even in the darkness.

"He could be bleeding to death somewhere," Lydia said.

It was going on eleven o'clock. Quist had been missing now for eight hours. The shot had been heard by the Tinker boy about three-thirty. If Quist had received a bleeding wound, they were looking for a dead man.

"The gunshot may have nothing to do with what's happened to him," Garvey said.

"What then?"

"He may have gotten tired of you and taken off with some other chick," Garvey said.

They laughed a little hysterically. They both knew that was the one thing that had not happened.

CHAPTER FOUR

Earlier . . .

Quist tried to make an assessment of his situation. It was now only about four o'clock and he'd left Lydia just about an hour ago. There was no reason why she should have begun to feel any anxiety about him. He couldn't expect—nor should his captors expect—any sort of search for him right away. And yet Smith and Jones—nothing else to call them—seemed to be working under high tension. Quist's appearance on the scene had thrown some kind of serious monkey wrench into a careful plan.

From the snatches of conversation, Quist was able to make some guesses. The two men had thought they would be safe in this camp with their prisoner for at least a week. The pop-singer owner was scheduled to be gone for that length of time. Quist's appearance, following the unhappy water spaniel, created a danger for them. The snarling dog had drawn Jarvis-Jones out of the house, his curiosity too great. He'd come face to face with Quist. Quist could identify him, couldn't be allowed to walk away. But certainly, within a short space of time, people would come looking for a missing man. Inquiries would be made at all the camps, and any that weren't occupied, like this one, would certainly be entered and searched. A search would reveal not only Quist but the girl. "Big money—big power," Smith had said. The chances were the kidnapping was already news. Quist and Lydia hadn't bothered to look at television or listen to the news on radio since they'd arrived at Altman's camp, but in all probability the local people, who would do the searching once they were alerted by Lydia, would know about it, would recognize the girl, Tiana, for whoever she really was.

Smith had mentioned a CB radio, which he obviously had in the next room. He had contacted someone named Dixon, who was coming to take them all away in a helicopter. Everything depended on the arrival of the helicopter before search parties appeared on the scene. One thing was certain. Smith and his partner Jones, whose first or last real name—Jarvis—had slipped out, were professionals. They were no wild-eyed terrorists.

Preparations for the evacuation were meticulous. Everything in the cabin must be left exactly as they had found it. If the place was searched after they had left it, there must be no signs that anybody had occupied it in the pop singer's absence. The kitchen, which Quist never saw, was apparently their main problem. They had prepared food there. Every trace of it must be eliminated, garbage taken out somewhere and buried, china and silverware put back exactly where they found it. Quist could hear almost childish arguments about where pots and pans had been located. Smith, his cold grey eyes narrowed, checked out the room where Quist and Tiana were held. The girl watched, evidently not understanding what was in the works. Smith kept looking at his wristwatch. Time must be dragging for him.

There was, Quist thought, another touchy factor for Smith and Jones. A helicopter, arriving in daylight, would certainly be seen, remarked on. It could touch down in the open space in front of the cabin, but the transfer of the prisoners and equipment must be made in a very great hurry. Search parties could be close by; occupants of other camps might come looking to see what a helicopter was doing down in the woods.

Smith put it into words to Quist: "You could make things very difficult for us, Quist," he said.

"I wish I knew how," Quist said.

"When the copter gets here," Smith said, "we'll all have to move on the double." He glanced at the handcuffs that anchored Quist to the big chair. "We'll have to turn you loose for that operation. You could hang back, force us to drag you. That would be unfortunate."

"And risky, I imagine," Quist said.

"Very risky. We have no desire to complicate things with a murder," Smith said. "But if Jarvis has to do to you what he did to the dog, he will. You have a chance, Quist, when this is all over, of walking away a free man. But if you try to complicate things for us any more than you have, we simply can't waste time on excess baggage. I would regret having to take steps. Jarvis, however, might enjoy it."

"Who is the girl?" Quist asked.

"You don't really know?"

"No."

"You didn't see the news on TV or listen to the radio this morning?"

"No."

"I know the newspapers that reach this neck of the woods wouldn't have had it," Smith said.

"I haven't seen a newspaper. I came up here to get away from a screwed-up world for a few days."

"You don't speak any Arab dialects?"

"No."

"So you don't understand what the girl was trying to tell you."

"No. Perhaps her name. Tiana?"

Smith smiled. "Close, but no cigar," he said.

"So much for sign language," Quist said.

Smith took that anxious look at his watch again. The lines at the corners of his eyes and mouth seemed to deepen. "There'll be no time to discuss it when the moment comes, Quist," he said. "Jarvis will unlock the cuffs and you will move, just as fast as you can, to the copter. If you stall, or make a run for it, that will be that. Understand?"

"What about the girl? She can't understand what you're telling her."

"What would you say—about a hundred pounds?" Smith asked. "We'll carry her, bodily, or drag her by the hair of her head. Just concern yourself about yourself, Quist."

From one of the back rooms came the sound of a mechanical voice, repeating some kind of call number. Smith turned and hurried off. It must be the CB radio with some message from the copter.

Quist looked at his watch. Twenty minutes past six. Surely Lydia would have become alarmed by now. Jarvis-Jones appeared from the kitchen, where he'd been cleaning things up. He took his gun out of its holster and examined it. He toyed with it, hefting it as though handling it was a pleasure. A man who made his living with a gun, Quist thought.

Quist, with his free hand, got another of his thin cigars out of his breast pocket, dug out his lighter, and got his smoke going. He reached down toward his pocket with the lighter.

Smith came out of the back room. He was carrying a CB radio. "About ten minutes," he said. "Everything ready?"

"Kitchen's clean," Jones said. The black glasses surveyed the room. "Nothing out of place here."

"The girl's purse," Smith said sharply.

Jones went over to the table next to the girl, picked up her small bag, and stuffed it in his jacket pocket. In the distance

Quist heard the sound of the helicopter's motors. He considered the possibilities. Both Smith and Jones were uptight. Jones was trigger happy. This wasn't the time to try heroics. Maybe later, in some other place, the climate would be more promising. He looked at the girl and tried encouraging her with a smile.

The copter roared overhead. It was coming down.

"Now!" Smith said.

Jarvis came over to Quist and unfastened the half of the handcuff that was attached to the chair. He gave Quist his white-toothed smile. "Don't try tempting me, buster," he said.

"Count on it," Quist said.

Smith opened the front door and a blast of air from the copter's propeller blades swept into the room.

"Go!" Smith said.

Quist, his legs feeling cramped, moved quickly across the room and out the front door. He knew that Jones was directly behind him. The copter was down, the passenger door open, a small set of steps lowered. Leaves and dust blew into Quist's face. He reached the copter and climbed the steps into its cabin. Jones, right behind him, grinned.

"That's a good boy," he said.

The girl, Tiana, had offered no resistance. She preceded Smith into the cabin and sat down in a little jump seat next to Quist. Smith took the seat next to the pilot, whose face was hidden behind a flying helmet and goggles. Jones crouched behind them, his .44 aimed casually at Quist and Tiana. The steps were retracted, the cabin door closed. The engine roared and the copter began to lift off.

Quist looked out the side window. Nothing. No one. He leaned back in his seat and was astonished to feel ice-cold fingers gripping his hand. He turned and saw Tiana staring up at him with her wide, frightened eyes.

He couldn't tell her what was on his mind, even if he could speak her language. He had left something behind in the pop singer's cabin. His monogrammed lighter had not gone back into his pocket that last time. Instead he had slipped it down between the cushion and the arm of the chair to which he'd been handcuffed. If somebody found it, it might help solve a puzzle.

CHAPTER FIVE

The hardest part of getting through the night was doing nothing. Since Garvey's arrival at the camp, there had been no word from Sergeant Stryker or anyone else in the search party. It was well after midnight. The most difficult part about it, Lydia thought, was that there was nothing to talk about. You couldn't reminisce about Julian as though he were dead. There wasn't even the smallest detail explaining his disappearance that you could chew on. He had just gone for a walk. There hadn't been anything on his mind except to stretch his legs. Garvey had wanted to go out to join the search party but Lydia had persuaded him that he'd be no help out there in the dark.

"I could wind up with both of you lost!" she said. She laughed as she said it, not wanting to admit to Dan how desperately she needed him here with her, someone familiar, totally dependable; someone who could make decisions if there were decisions to make.

It wasn't possible to think of anything but disaster. It wasn't as if someone had missed a plane or a train, failed to arrive at an airport or a depot. A man could have an accident driving from one place to another in a car, not be able to find a telephone, or be carted off to an emergency ward in some hospital. There was no explanation for what had happened to Julian. The woods here were not impenetrable. In the half hour between the time he'd started on his walk and the time Jerry Tinker had heard the gunshot, Julian couldn't have gotten very far away. The woods were dotted with cabins according to Joe Wellman and the police. He could almost have stood still and called out for help and been heard. There was, according to Wellman, no bad place for a fall. If he had tripped over something, knocked himself out, broken a leg, he would surely have come to in less than nine hours and crawled for help or shouted for help. In the last five hours the woods had been alive with searchers. If Julian was conscious, he must surely have heard them.

So they always came back to the gunshot, which could have silenced Julian forever. A fall into some thick bushes, into some declivity in the ground. Silence because he was dead. In the darkness, searchers could easily overlook a motionless body. In the morning, in daylight, extra searchers would find him.

They didn't, couldn't, talk about what they would do without him; what would become of the business, which was their lives; how they, and so many others, would reorganize the techniques of living. All they could do was wait for the news that would spell the end of their particular world, so secure, so glamorous, so joyful until that moment when Julian had decided to go for a short walk.

There was liquor in the cabin but neither Lydia nor Garvey wanted a drink, though each of them offered to make one for the other. In case there was something to be done, they needed all of their faculties at their sharpest.

"To do what?" Lydia asked, when Garvey, for the tenth time, refused a drink, explaining why.

"To welcome the stretcher-bearers," he said grimly.

She had made coffee—and then made a second pot. Small talk was impossible. Sleep was impossible. Garvey had taken to pacing up and down the room. It seemed he had walked miles when he glanced at his watch, turned to the transistor radio on the center table, switched it on. There was a world outside somewhere.

"—the fourth bell will mark the exact hour," an announcer's voice said. There were four bells, the last one the loudest. "It is now exactly two o'clock. The stories we will cover in the next half hour include Mayor Koch's visit to Washington, where he talked about city finances with President Carter; a murder and kidnapping outside the posh Hotel Beaumont in Manhattan; all the sports scores and racing results; a report by Don Dilloway on places to dine and entertainments to enjoy; Bob Shaw on the summer feeding of wild birds; and Hamilton Warner's interview with Norma Burton, actress of the week, talking about her new film, *The Sniper.* Mayor Koch went to Washington again yesterday, hat in hand, to ask the President for help with New York City's uncertain finances. The Mayor had lunch at the White House with the President, but there were no positive statements made after their meeting. 'The President was sympathetic to our problems,' Mr. Koch said, 'but as yet—' "

"Can you wait to hear about feeding wild birds?" Garvey asked Lydia, sourly.

"The big story of the day in New York," the announcer went on, "was the brutal murder of a well-known British diplomat, David Peters, outside the posh Hotel Beaumont, and the kidnapping of Miss Tatiana Feydhev, daughter of the millionaire oil tycoon from the Middle East, Rhaman Feydhev. Mr. Peters had escorted Miss Feydhev to the theater night before last. They returned to the hotel, where she was staying with her father, shortly after midnight, in a taxi. As the couple got out of the taxi, several unidentified men seized Miss Feydhev and dragged her down the street. Mr. Peters, a reserve officer in the British Royal Air Force, attempted to rescue her and was shot twice, in the face and in the chest, by one of the kidnappers. He was pronounced dead on arrival at Bellevue Hospital.

"The doorman at the Beaumont, Henry Waters, was unable to supply a description of the kidnappers. Just before the taxi carrying Miss Feydhev and Mr. Peters arrived at the Beaumont, Waters had been called to a service phone just inside the front doors. When Waters answered the phone there was no one on the other end. Police believe Waters was called away by an ally of the kidnappers so that he would not be outside on the sidewalk when the violence took place.

"Manhattan Homicide and the FBI are both working on the case, but so far there have been no statements from either source. Agent Frank Rubek, FBI, in charge of the kidnapping investigation, made it clear that until the kidnappers undertake to negotiate with Miss Feydhev's father there will be no information forthcoming.

"Rhaman Feydhev, the girl's father, is reported to be one of the richest men in the world. Like many oil tycoons in the Middle East, he has invested huge sums in American business and industry. He has refused any interviews with the press. His suite at the Beaumont is being guarded by police and FBI agents while he waits for demands from the abductors of his lovely daughter. Tatiana Feydhev is twenty years old and her name has been linked romantically with several eligible bachelors, including the late Mr. Peters. A State Department source, asked if there could be any political implications in the tragedy, simply commented that where so much wealth is involved 'politics can't be far behind.' It is believed—"

Garvey switched off the radio. "Cockeyed world," he said

angrily. "Crazy creeps with guns. Will nobody ever wake up?"

He was thinking about a gunshot in the woods, not the cutting down of David Peters outside the Beaumont.

CHAPTER SIX

He called himself Cannikin. It came from Robert Browning's "When the liquor's out, why clink the cannikin?" He had no idea what a cannikin was, unless it was an empty glass or mug. But he needed a professional name and it just came to him off a page he was reading. His real name was Wilfred Winterbottom. He needed something else to appear before the public with his guitar and his folk songs. So it was Cannikin. He played obscure saloons and night spots, going nowhere in particular. Finally he got a chance to make some recordings and he was suddenly famous. Three gold records in the space of a couple of years. He could call his own shots, live in any kind of luxury he chose.

What he chose was relatively simple, a camp on Lake Toromog. Wilfred Winterbottom had grown up a country boy, and Cannikin had lost none of that taste for the woods, the streams, the quiet. It was a blessed relief from shrieking girls in huge auditoriums, from autograph hunters who tore at his clothes, from agents and publicity sharks who wanted a share of his success. Records became the main source of his income, but he had to make enough public appearances to keep his image alive. He would make those appearances, maybe one a month; and there would be recording sessions, maybe once every two months.

Girls, and even older women, hunted him as if he were the sex symbol of all time. He could have had any one of thousands for the asking. But Wilfred Winterbottom, who had become Cannikin, was a loner. He liked to be alone. He had just one companion, a springer spaniel named Charlie—Charlie Brown, a name he'd picked out of a famous comic strip. At the camp Charlie Brown never left Cannikin's heels, slept on the foot of his bed, looked at him endlessly with adoring eyes. Cannikin carried on long conversations with Charlie, certain that the dog understood every word of what was said to him. It was a genuine love affair.

Cannikin and Charlie had one problem, the necessity for Cannikin to go away for his recording sessions and his personal appearances. In the beginning, when Charlie was quite young, Cannikin took him along. But hotel rooms, shrieking crowds, and sidewalk gutters for his necessities were a misery for the dog. He endured, but he was an unhappy character. Cannikin decided he must find a place to leave Charlie at the lake when he went on his trips. He located an elderly spinster, living just down the road from Joe Wellman's place, who had just lost a dog of her own, didn't want a new permanent attachment, but was delighted to care for Charlie Brown while Cannikin was away.

He tried it. When he came back Charlie was overjoyed to see him, but he said good-bye, politely, to Mrs. Woodruff. When the time came for the next trip, Charlie was perfectly content to go back to the widow lady. He knew now that Cannikin would come back for him.

On the morning of the day that Lydia and Quist arrived at Pat Altman's camp, Cannikin was scheduled to do a week of performances in Philadelphia. The offer had come out of the blue from a producer he didn't know, but the money was too tempting to refuse. Normally, he didn't go away from the lake for so long. He notified Mrs. Woodruff that he would be bringing Charlie to her. He told Charlie, who seemed to understand. He let Charlie out for a run before it was time to go.

Charlie didn't come back.

It was unheard-of. Cannikin went looking for his dog, without success. It finally occurred to him that Charlie had known that he was headed for Mrs. Woodruff's and taken off on his own. When Cannikin drove to Mrs. Woodruff's in his jeep he found, unhappily, that Charlie hadn't been as psychic as he had hoped.

Mrs. Woodruff cheered him. She would go up to the cabin later and find Charlie. Cannikin had to leave. Success had made it possible to have a small plane of his own, and he drove to the local airport and took off in it for Philadelphia.

As soon as he got to his hotel he phoned Mrs. Woodruff. She had been to the cabin but there was no sign of Charlie.

Cannikin, in a state of intense anxiety, did his thing for the squealing girls in Philadelphia. All he could think about was Charlie. He didn't have to appear again until the next evening. At first light the next morning he took off in his plane and flew back to the airport near the lake. He drove to the cabin.

No Charlie.

He began to search and found his friend almost at once, in a clump of bushes only a few yards from the cabin. He found what was left of his friend. He saw the mangled leg with the steel trap still attached to it. He saw the head that looked as if something had exploded inside the animal's brain.

He sat down in the grass, took the bloodied remains in his lap, and wept.

After the storm of weeping was over, Cannikin picked up the dog's body and carried it into the cabin, putting it gently down on the foot of the bed, where Charlie had always slept.

Rage had taken charge and it shook Cannikin's whole body. He was a country boy and he knew something about gunshot wounds. This hadn't been inflicted by some hunter's shotgun.

He went into the kitchen to get a sharp pointed knife he used for cleaning fish. He spent a lot of time fishing when he was at the camp. The knife wasn't in the drawer where it belonged.

Frowning, he opened the next drawer. There was the knife. It was a small thing, but Cannikin was a man of rigid routines. He always put things in exactly the same place. He began to look around the kitchen. Saucers and coffee cups were stacked on the shelf next to the stove, cups on top of the saucers. He never left them that way. Saucers in one stack, cups beside them was the way he always did it. He opened the cupboard next to the shelves. The two-pound can of Maxwell House coffee was on the top shelf, not the middle shelf.

Someone had been here.

He took the pointed knife and went back into the bedroom. He sat down on the edge of the bed and stroked the rigid body of his dead friend.

"I'm sorry, Charlie," he said softly, "but I have to do it, boy."

He took a deep breath and probed the shattered head with the knife. He was looking for a bullet.

He found it.

CHAPTER SEVEN

With the first grey of morning light in the east, Sergeant Stryker, one sleeve of his soiled uniform torn, where it had caught on something, came out of the woods and across the clearing to the Altman camp. He looked a very tired man. Lydia and Garvey were in the open door before the sergeant reached it. They didn't have to speak their question.

"Nothing so far, Miss Morton," Stryker said, "which you have to look at as good news of a sort."

"Why?" Garvey asked, his dark face set hard.

Lydia introduced the two men. Stryker had been long gone on the search when Garvey arrived.

"No answer is better than the wrong answer," Stryker said.

"Coffee, Sergeant?" Lydia asked.

"I sure could use it, Miss Morton."

Stryker sat at the table in the little dining alcove gratefully drinking the coffee Lydia brought him. Without asking, she was preparing bacon and eggs for all of them. Stryker leaned back in his chair finally, and lit a cigarette.

"It's pretty tough out there in the dark," he said. "All you've got is your torch. You keep swinging it around, but you could miss something three feet away from you. We should be able to make pretty certain in the next hour or so."

"Why?" Garvey asked. His only word, it seemed.

"Couple of dozen men due here from town as soon as it's really light," Stryker said. "They'll cover every inch of the place within a couple of miles. He can't have gotten much further than that, just walking."

"You base that on the gunshot the Tinker boy heard?" Garvey asked. "His statement as to the time he heard it?"

Stryker nodded. "Only thing we have to go on," he said.

"Only reasonable explanation as to what happened. Shot by accident."

"Maybe I don't buy that," Garvey said.

"Because you don't want to, Mr. Garvey?"

"Perhaps."

"Is there something no one has told me?" Stryker asked. "Is there some reason he could have taken off, voluntarily, without saying anything to Miss Morton or anyone else?"

"No," Lydia said from where she was putting strips of bacon to drain on some paper toweling while she started eggs.

"Then we can only think—" Stryker shrugged.

"A fall," Garvey suggested.

"And unconscious for fifteen hours? If he's in the radius of where we've been looking, even though we haven't spotted him, he must have heard us if he was conscious. Even if he can't move, he could have called to us. One way or the other it's a pretty bleak picture, Mr. Garvey." The sergeant seemed to brighten as Lydia served him bacon and eggs and toast. Garvey ignored the plate brought for him.

Stryker ate a few mouthfuls. "Boy, this is delicious, Miss Morton. If there's just a spot more coffee—?"

They let Stryker work the edge off his appetite. He was a very hungry man. Finally he began to fill them in a little.

"There are thirteen cabins on this side of the lake," he said. "You wouldn't think it to look out the window, but it's really quite thickly populated out there. Twelve of those cabins are occupied right now, were occupied yesterday afternoon. We've talked to people in every one of those twelve places. No one has seen Quist. He didn't ask anyone for directions or help, if he got lost. Three people heard the gunshot Jerry Tinker reported. They all place it at sometime between three and four. Since hunting is prohibited up here, a gunshot isn't usual."

"And only three people heard it?"

"You know how it is, Mr. Garvey. You hear a sound that isn't usual. Since guns aren't allowed, you think maybe it's a car backfiring—maybe one of the power launches on the lake. The three people who say they heard a gun are three guys with war records. They know a gunshot when they hear it."

Garvey was still hoping. "What about the thirteenth cabin?"

"Belongs to a fellow named Willie Winterbottom," Stryker said. "He's some kind of a pop singer. Country western, I guess. Calls himself Cannikin. He's away, doing a week of personal appearances in Philadelphia."

"Cannikin is a very big deal in the music world," Lydia said.

Any hope was a hope. "Did you search his cabin, Stryker?" Garvey asked.

"No. It was closed up. People knew where he'd gone."

"Suppose Julian stumbled on the cabin, was hurt, went in—passed out?" Garvey suggested.

Stryker put down his fork, reluctantly. "Didn't occur to me, I'm afraid," he said. "I mean, the place was shut up."

"Let's go," Garvey said. At least it was something to do.

There was a logging road that led up the hill to Cannikin's place. They took Garvey's car. As they approached the cabin, they saw a jeep parked outside.

"That's Cannikin's," Stryker said. "He's not supposed to be back for another five or six days."

As Garvey parked his car the door to the cabin opened and Cannikin faced them. He wore his blond hair long. Women used to cut their hair that way and call it a "boyish bob."

"I was just about to come looking for you, Sergeant," Cannikin said.

"When did you get back?" Stryker asked.

"Less than an hour ago," Cannikin said. "There's been all hell going on here, Sergeant. I—"

"We're looking for a missing man," Garvey interrupted. "Is he in there with you?"

"I haven't seen any man," Cannikin said. "But somebody shot my dog, and if I can lay hands on the sonofabitch—"

"When was he shot?" Stryker asked.

"Sometime yesterday, I'd guess." Cannekin told them the story of Charlie Brown's disappearance just as he was about to take off for Philadelphia. Told them how he'd had to go, had heard from Mrs. Woodruff that Charlie hadn't come back to the cabin, and that early this morning he'd flown back from Philadelphia. "Charlie was just a few yards off the path down there," he said. "The poor old boy was caught in some kind of trap. Who does any trapping up here, Sergeant? Place is posted!"

Stryker shook his head.

"Charlie tried to chew his leg out of it. Damn near succeeded. Then somebody shot him in the head."

Garvey was fond of animals. He could sympathize with Cannikin's obvious anger and grief. But he was fonder of Julian, and he felt a new hope. No one had reported hearing more than one shot. If the one shot had killed Cannikin's dog, then Julian hadn't been the target, accidental or on purpose.

"I dug the bullet out of Charlie's head," Cannikin said. He reached in his pocket and produced the slug. "Looks like it came from an oversize handgun." He handed it to Stryker.

"Looks like a .44 caliber cannon," Stryker said.

"Somebody's been in the cabin," Cannikin said.

"How do you know?"

"Things out of place," Cannikin said. "Somebody made coffee, put the can back in the wrong place. Used several cups and saucers, washed them but put them back wrong. Other things. Come in and see for yourself."

The cabin looked neat as a pin, except for the gruesome corpse of the dog on the foot of the bed.

Cannikin glanced at Lydia's white, strained face and bent down to cover the remains with a blanket. He patted the dead dog before he covered him.

"I don't like to go looking for things when I want them," Cannikin said. "My mother used to kid me, say I was an old maid, because everything had a place and I'd raise hell if it was put back different. I told you about the coffee and the cups and saucers. There was a knife, the one I wanted to use to dig for the bullet in Charlie's head. It was in the wrong drawer. Somebody had to misplace those things, not me. And in the bathroom—" Cannekin picked up a piece of tissue he'd put down on the table. "In the basket under the washbasin. It's got lipstick on it." He held up the red-stained tissue. "I figure some kids knew I was away, figured this would be a great place to make out in. Had themselves a time, making out, coffee, the works. But they didn't know just how to put things back. So help me, if I find them and they shot my dog—"

"Maybe it was meant to be a kindness," Stryker said.

"How do you mean?"

"Charlie was bad hurt from the trap," the sergeant said. "Maybe half crazy trying to eat his way out of it. Maybe they thought shooting him was the only human thing to do."

"Jesus Christ!" Garvey shouted.

He had sat down in a big armchair while Cannikin told his story. There was something lumpy under him and he reached down to see what it was. Now he was holding out his hand, and lying in the palm was Quist's gold monogrammed lighter.

"Lydia, isn't this—?"

"Oh my God!" she said.

"You gave it to him for his last birthday!"

"What are you talking about?" Stryker asked.

"This lighter! It's Quist's! He was here in this cabin, Sergeant. Cute bastard left it here for us to find, I think."

Lydia, who never cried, cried for the second time in the last few hours, this time with almost unbearable relief. There was, at least, some small reason to hope. The thirteenth cabin had provided that small reason. Lucky thirteen!

CHAPTER EIGHT

Almost twelve hours before Garvey found Quist's lighter where it had been left in Cannikin's cabin, the helicopter carrying Quist, the girl he knew only as Tiana, and the two men with the unlikely names of Smith and Jones, headed north along the ridge of the Berkshire hills. Two hours more of daylight, Quist estimated. He knew the country below them moderately well. He had never had a sky view of it before, but he had traveled the roads heading for southern Vermont and a marvelous golf course in Manchester, where he had played in several invitational tournaments during summer holidays from college and later when he was first starting in business on his own. One of his first clients had been the eccentric owner of a chain of hamburger joints, who refused to discuss business anywhere except on the Ekwanok golf course in Manchester. He had closed a whopping deal that put Julian Quist Associates on the map on the back-breaking par 5 seventh hole at Ekwanok, where his client had just scored a horrifying eleven and thrown his golf clubs into the bushes.

As the light began to fade drastically, Quist caught a glimpse of the Bennington Monument. Manchester, his old hangout, was only about twenty miles further north. They would be passing over it, Quist thought, just about the time the daylight would be entirely gone.

There was no chance for conversation in the noisy cabin of the chopper, even if there had been anyone to talk to. The girl, with whom he couldn't communicate, had sat with her icy fingers linked in his until she seemed to relax and her hand began to feel warm. Jones, the man with the black glasses, played with his gun, aiming it here, aiming it there. Occasionally he smiled at Quist, as if to remind him that he could blow a hole in him through which a truck could be driven.

Darkness settled in, except for a reddish glow on the western horizon, which probably couldn't be seen from ground level. "Red sky at night, sailor's delight." Tomorrow would be a fine day. Quist wondered whether he would be around to see it. Jarvis-Jones seemed all too eager for some kind of action.

The chopper began to circle. Looking down, Quist saw a tiny light. It was being waved upward in consistent circles at the chopper. Somebody was locating a landing spot for the pilot. The descent began.

The girl, Tiana, sat straight up in her seat, and once more her hand gripped Quist's. Smith, the grey-haired one, sitting up front with the pilot, reached back and touched Jones's shoulder. He pointed down with his forefinger and Jones nodded. He stopped playing games and pointed the gun steadily at Quist.

The chopper touched down and the motor was switched off. The silence was more deafening than the noise had been. Quist looked out and saw at least a dozen lights, evidently coming from the windows of a large house. The chopper door opened, the steps were let down.

"Out you go, buster," Jones said, pointing with his gun. The girl didn't want to let go of Quist's hand. He gave her a reassuring smile, a reassurance he didn't feel, and gently disengaged her fingers. He went down the steps to the ground, his head bent to keep from banging against the top of the door frame. Three men waited for him at ground level. All of them were armed with handguns. Quist knew that if he saw them again he would know them all. It was disturbing, because the more people he could identify later the less chance there was of there being any "later." Jones, coming up just behind them, clamped one end of the handcuffs on Quist's right wrist and the other on his own.

"No hide-and-seek in the dark," Jones said. He pressed his gun against Quist's side. "Step lively, partner," he said.

The girl and Smith were just behind, immediately surrounded by the three men who had been waiting. The chopper pilot came out last, taking off his helmet and goggles. Quist would know him again. Back at the cabin on the lake someone had mentioned the name "Dixon."

They were, it appeared, on a wide lawn facing a large brick house, with white colonial columns framing a front door that stood open. Beyond it was a wide entrance hall, warmly lit. Someone with taste and money owned this place, Quist thought.

Leading up from the entrance hall was a beautiful curving stairway and Jones indicated that Quist was to go up. No one else appeared inside the house. They climbed the stairs, went down a wide hall, and into a room at the far end. Jones turned on a light switch just inside the door and Quist found himself in a charmingly appointed bedroom. There was an antique canopied bed, bureau, table, chairs, all antique Colonial. A door stood open to a white-tiled bathroom.

Jones unlocked the handcuffs and backed off, slipping them in his pocket but keeping his gun on Quist.

"Suit your lordship?" He asked.

"Nice room," Quist said.

"Time for a little talk about the facts of life," Jones said. "So far as I know there hasn't been any decision about what the hell to do with you, Quist. But let's go into geography first. Those windows open onto a flower garden below. A desperate man might risk jumping. Only one floor up. But there are two men waiting down there for just that to happen. The door to this room will be locked, but if you should try to break out there'll be someone in the hall waiting to blow your handsome head off. Clear?"

"Clear."

"I imagine you could stand something to eat, maybe a drink."

"Specially a drink," Quist said.

"You can't exactly ring for the butler," Jones said, "but someone will be along to take care of you. I don't want you to misunderstand for a minute, Quist. Escape is impossible. You may not get to live anyway, but you certainly won't if you try to make a break for it."

"Where are we?" Quist asked.

Jones grinned at him. "Never-never land," he said.

There was one thing in the room that jarred with the antique furnishings. It was a cabinet-size television set.

"I don't suppose that thing works," Quist said.

"Everything in this house works," Jones said.

"Any reason I shouldn't turn it on?" Quist asked. "Help to pass the time."

"No reason I know of," Jones said. He glanced at his wristwatch. "Catch the nine o'clock news and you may understand better why you're here. And why you'd better be a good boy."

Jones went out and Quist heard the door lock falling into place. He hesitated for a moment and then went over and switched on the television set. It took a moment for the screen to clear and then, astonishingly, Quist found himself looking at a familiar face. A man and a woman were sitting on either side of a table. The man, the theater and movie critic for the network, was concluding an interview with Miss Norma Burton, the actress. Miss Burton was an old friend and client of Quist's.

"And so," the interviewer said, "this concludes my interview with Norma Burton, who will be my guest all this week. Her new film, *The Sniper,* will be seen all over the country, beginning ten days from now. Thank you, Norma, for being with me."

"A pleasure," Miss Burton said.

Quist had the absurd notion to say "Hi, Norma!"

"And now to the nine o'clock news." The camera switched to a well-known newscaster. "Still nothing new on the kidnapping and murder, which took place just after midnight night before last outside the Hotel Beaumont in Manhattan. The kidnapping of Miss Tatiana Feydhev and the murder of her escort, Mr. David Peters, is still a complete mystery as far as the general public is concerned. The FBI and New York City's Homicide Squad are still not giving out any statements. It still isn't known whether the kidnappers have made any demands on Rhaman Feydhev, the girl's millionaire oil-tycoon father. Feydhev remains in seclusion in his suite at the Beaumont, guarded by police and FBI agents. It is understandable that his daughter's safety is more important to Feydhev than satisfying the curiosity of the press.

"Homicide is equally secretive about the murder of David Peters, who attempted to rescue Miss Feydhev from her kidnappers on the sidewalk outside the Beaumont. He was shot twice, once in the face, once in the chest, and was dead on arrival at the hospital. As far as we know, it all happened so quickly that there are no witnesses who have anything of consequence to report. Now, for a report on the hearings in Washington on the alleged bribery of congressmen by a Korean businessman, we switch to—"

Quist shut off the set. Tatiana Feydhev! He tried to remember what he knew about Rhaman Feydhev. Oil. The world was wrapped up in oil problems and Feydhev controlled a large segment of that indispensable commodity. His wealth was unlimited. The demands that could be made on him for the return of his daughter were astronomical. That girl, hidden in some other room down the hall, could bring almost any price that was asked. One thing was certain. Someone who walked into the situation as Quist had, threatening exposure, was just a pawn on the chessboard, not worth protecting for an instant. Quist wondered why they had kept him alive so long.

Somebody opened the door lock and Quist turned to see a black man in a servant's white coat come in carrying a tray. Behind him was one of the men Quist had seen when the chopper landed, gun in hand.

The black man put down the tray and removed a linen napkin that covered what was on the tray. Cold roast beef, a mixed green salad, rolls and butter, a generous slice of apple pie, and a pot of coffee.

The black man smiled at Quist and pantomimed the gesture of drinking something.

"What's the matter?" Quist asked. "Cat got your tongue?"

Then he went into something like shock as the black man opened his mouth and pointed. The black man had no tongue.

CHAPTER NINE

Lieutenant Mark Kreevich of Manhattan Homicide was a slim, wiry man, sandy haired, with bright blue eyes and an intense manner. He was the new breed of cop, college educated, law degree. He was a man whose life was dedicated to law and order, not the cliché kind brought to the fore in election years by our politicians. He believed in a society in which people could live in some other way than on the defensive. He resented the fact, and often gave voice to it, that in his job he never got involved until after the crime was committed. There should be a system in which prevention came ahead of solution.

Kreevich was a cultivated man. He could talk about music, or art, or theater, or the ballet. But, if you knew him, you knew that his chief concern was the job, whatever case he might be handling. "A two-track mind," Quist once said of him.

By the strangest of coincidences, Kreevich and Quist were close friends. Crime had brought them together, friendship had kept them together. The second day after the murder of David Peters and the kidnapping of Tatiana Feydhev, Kreevich had only one thing on his mind: to find the murderer or murderers of Peters; and, hopefully, to uncover some lead to the kidnappers. On the morning of that second day, he had no idea that Quist was missing. It wasn't yet a news item. He had no reason at all to think about Quist or to be concerned about him.

The murder of David Peters was the kind of case Kreevich hated to handle. The connection to the kidnapping meant the involvement of the FBI, meant trying to make what amounted to two different investigations walk hand in hand.

Anyone with any heart had to be primarily concerned with the safe return of Tatiana Feydhev. She was, one hoped, alive. Her old man could afford to meet any kind of ransom demand if the demand was for money alone. But, in this day and age, with a man like Rhaman Feydhev involved up to his armpits in political and economic schemings and dealings, one had to expect that this kidnapping would follow a world pattern. The demand would be for money and something else; something Rhaman Reydhev might not find it so easy to give. There could be demands for political concessions, the release of political prisoners, transfers of power.

On the third morning after the kidnapping, Kreevich sat in his office at police headquarters, in a huddle with Frank Rubek, the FBI agent in charge of that aspect of the case. Kreevich knew Rubek and respected him, but he resented having to handle his own case under wraps imposed by the FBI.

Not that Kreevich had very much to go on. The night—or early morning—of the crime, Tatiana Feydhev and David Peters had gone to see a production of *A Chorus Line,* a popular musical in its second year on Broadway. In spite of Feydhev's money, there was no particular security surrounding the girl's activities. David Peters was a responsible escort. One might have expected that after the theater Peters might have taken the girl to some sort of night spot for a drink and further entertainment. Since neither Peters nor the girl was available to say what their plans had been, Kreevich could only make guesses. They could have decided to end their evening with the theater. They could have stopped somewhere near the theater for a drink before returning to the Beaumont. In the Beaumont was the Blue Lagoon Room, one of the better late night entertainment spots, and they could have been headed there. Tatiana Feydhev would then only have had to go upstairs to her suite when they'd had enough. Arriving at the hotel shortly after midnight in a taxi suggested they'd stopped somewhere after the final curtain of the musical. Kreevich hadn't been able to run that down so far. Not that it mattered much. The action had taken place on the sidewalk outside the hotel.

Henry Waters, the doorman at the Beaumont, had the first unusual bit of evidence to offer. A few minutes after midnight the night bell captain had come out of the hotel to tell Waters he was wanted on the phone.

"It was not too unusual," Waters told Kreevich. "We have all kinds of very rich people, statesmen from the United Nations, staying with us. They want special service. I supposed someone wanted a taxi waiting for him, or perhaps one of the hotel's limousines."

"Not a personal call?" Kreevich asked.

"I don't get personal calls," Waters said. "I have no family. Any friends I have know better than to call me when I'm on the job. Anyway, I went inside to the phone that's located just by the front doors. When I picked up the phone and answered, the line was dead. The switchboard operator came on, told me there'd been a call for me, but whoever it was had hung up. 'Hang on,' she said, 'it may have been an accidental cutoff and they'll call back.' "

"Did you ask her if it was a call from inside the hotel or from the outside?" Kreevich asked.

"Not just then," Waters said. "I took it for granted it was a guest from inside. I waited, maybe a minute—two minutes —for the call to come back. And then I heard the gunshots."

Kreevich knew, now, that the call had come from outside the hotel. A man's voice had asked the switchboard operator to connect him with the doorman at the Fifth Avenue entrance to the hotel. She had assumed someone wanted the doorman to arrange for a hotel limousine to pick him up somewhere. Not an unheard-of circumstance.

There had been, Waters thought, three gunshots. Two of them were accounted for, bullets buried in the unfortunate Peters's head and chest. Kreevich had not been able to come up with a third bullet, which had missed its target. There might not have been a third bullet. In the excitement Waters might not have been accurate about what he heard.

Waters ran out onto the sidewalk. He saw Tatiana Feydhev being dragged into a car, black or dark blue he thought. His main attention was directed to the body lying a few yards down on the sidewalk. He'd rushed to Peters and knew instantly that he was dead, face blown away, big hole in his chest, dress shirt red with blood. The car with the Feydhev girl in it, along with at least two men, possibly three with the driver, had raced away.

"I just wasn't collected enough to get the license number," Waters said.

The driver of the taxi, who had brought the unfortunate couple to the hotel, was no use at all. He had been paid by Peters, a generous tip included. He had been rearranging his money, bills in a wallet, coins in a little change dispenser fastened to the dash. He heard the shots and glanced up into his rearview mirror. What was happening was going on behind him. He saw the girl being "wrestled" into a car. He didn't see Peters or what had happened to him. It was out of the mirror's range.

"Jesus, Lieutenant, I didn't get out to see what was cooking. With someone shooting? I just ducked down and sat tight."

"You didn't get a good look at the car with the girl in it?"

"No, sir. Dark, like black or dark blue, or dark green. Middle size, like a Chevy Nova. Something like that."

"And the men?"

"Hell, man, I was ducking."

There were two other useless witnesses. A man across the

A Review Copy of

DEADLY TRAP
by Hugh Pentecost

Publication Date:
November 6, 1978

Price: $6.95

This book is sent to you with our compliments. We would appreciate two copies of your review.

79 Madison Avenue, New York, N.Y. 10016

DODD MEAD

street by the park walking a dog. He'd heard the shots, saw a car race off. He hadn't had time to check the license or the make of the car. His attention was focused on the man lying on the sidewalk.

Another taxi driver, waiting for business outside the hotel, had been too busy ducking when he heard the shots to see anything. The park was across the street, no building there. No one could have seen anything from a building unless they were hanging out a window, looking down.

The only concrete evidence Kreevich really had took him nowhere. The medical examiner had removed the two bullets from David Peters's body. They had been fired from a .44 caliber handgun. Neither homicide nor the FBI had any record in their ballistics files of any other shots fired by that particular gun.

A Chorus Line, the play the victims had attended, was playing at the Shubert Theater on West 44th Street. Kreevich had men covering all the bars and night spots in the area. He believed Tatiana Feydhev and Peters had stopped somewhere for a drink after the performance, which ended before eleven. An hour and twenty minutes before they arrived at the Beaumont and disaster. The taxi driver had picked them up in the Times Square area a few minutes before twelve. They had spent time somewhere. The whole planning seemed so exact, Waters called away from his post at just the right time, it seemed certain to Kreevich that someone had been watching the couple. Someone in some bar might have noticed a man or men who seemed to take a special interest in them. So far nothing.

Frank Rubek, the FBI man, had even less to go on. He was a lanky, sandy-haired man, with a normally pleasant face. This morning he looked like a man who was waiting for a bomb to go off.

"It's unreal," he told Kreevich. "This is the third morning. Feydhev has heard from the kidnappers twice, but no demands. He has been assured that his daughter is safe and well. When they are ready to name the ransom they'll be in touch. Just that, no more. Usual warning about the police and the FBI."

"Telephone?"

"Yes. The first call came the morning of the first day. We weren't ready for it. The second came yesterday morning. That time Feydhev's phone in the Beaumont was monitored, tapped, bugged, the works. We have a tape of the call. Man. Ordinary voice, ordinary English speech. Feydhev had wondered about Arab terrorists. A lot of Arabs speak fluent English, most of them with a British accent. This guy could have been from anywhere in this neck of the woods, New York most likely. 'Keep cool. Ransom demands will be made in the near future. Your daughter is safe and well.' That call came from a public coin box on a street corner on Madison Avenue."

"Why would they wait so long to make their demands?" Kreevich asked. "The more time they give us, the better chance we have of getting onto them."

"My guess is they've taken her out of the country," Rubek said. "Waiting to have her safely tucked away somewhere we'll never find before they start to deal. The place may have some special significance to Feydhev when the time comes, a place controlled by enemies."

"He has enemies?"

"A guy with that much bread always has enemies," Rubek said.

The phone rang on Kreevich's desk. He answered and it was for Rubek. He handed the phone to the FBI man.

Rubek's end of the conversation went like this: "Rubek here. Yes—You what?—Yeah—Yeah—Lake Toromog? Where the hell is that?—Yes, I'm writing it down—Well, thanks. It's something for God sake."

Rubek put down the phone and looked at Kreevich. "You won't believe," he said. "Camp at a place called Lake Toromog in the Berkshires. Somebody shot a dog. Police looking for a man missing in the woods. A sergeant of state troopers named Stryker sent the bullet to ballistics. They checked with Washington. It came from the same gun that was used to murder David Peters. So we have to assume the killer, probably the kidnappers, are in that area."

Kreevich was on his feet. "What are we waiting for?" he asked.

Two and a half hours later Kreevich and Rubeck arrived at the state police barracks just outside the Lake Toromog area. Sergeant Stryker was waiting for them.

"You could have knocked me over with a feather when they told me my bullet matched up with others from that murder and kidnapping in the city," Stryker said. "Of course I didn't dream of that when I sent the thing in to the ballistics people. We had something else going here. A man missing. We were looking for him."

He told of going to Cannikin's cabin on the chance the missing man might have found his way there, wounded, hurt. Instead there was Cannikin, the dead dog, the evidence that someone had occupied the cabin, the tissue with lipstick on it, and eventually the missing man's lighter stuffed down in the upholstery of an armchair.

"Who is the missing man?" Kreevich asked.

"Fellow named Quist, Julian Quist. Big-shot public relations operator, I understand."

"For God sake!" Kreevich said.

"You know him, Lieutenant?"

"One of my best friends," Kreevich said. "Are any of his other friends up here?"

"A Miss Morton, a Mr. Garvey. Dan Garvey, used to be a great football player."

"I know. Where are they?"

"At Pat Altman's camp, or they might still be up at Cannikin's place."

"That's where we need to go," Rubek said. "It's only a guess, Lieutenant, but it sounds like your friend walked into a hornet's nest."

"No sign of where they went?" Kreevich asked Stryker.

"There was a helicopter seen over the lake about six-thirty yesterday afternoon," Stryker said. "Marks in the grass outside Cannikin's cabin make us think it put down there. Where it went after that, who knows."

"With Quist on board?"

"We haven't found him anywhere else," Stryker said. "Covered every inch of the woods."

CHAPTER TEN

The night before . . .

Periodically Quist tried his television set. The news remained static. Nothing new on the murder and the kidnapping. If Rhaman Feydhev had received demands from the kidnappers, no one was saying. Quist wondered when his name would come across the broadcaster's desk. He was enough of a name to make the news when it was known he was missing.

He had found it a little difficult to eat the supper the tongueless black man had brought him. The man, pointing to his empty mouth, had shaken him. But after that ghastly moment he had made it clear that what he wanted was some bourbon, ice, plain water. The black man, smiling, had gone away and returned with a full quart of bourbon, a silver cooler of ice, a cut-glass flagon of water. This was no third-rate establishment. Quist made himself a stiff drink and felt momentarily better. But only momentarily. The more he tried to assess his situation the less he liked it. Just how bad it was, was made clear to him a little after midnight. The door to his room was unlocked and two men came in. One of them was Jarvis-Jones, black glasses glittering in the artificial light, gun hanging loosely in his right hand. The other was new to Quist, a rather handsome, dark-haired man, wearing a blue blazer, light-grey slacks, and a wine-red sports shirt, open at the throat. He was tanned to almost a mahogany brown.

"My name is Brooks Elliot," the man said, his speech cultivated. "This is my house. I trust your supper and the liquor I had sent were satisfactory."

"The only thing that would be satisfactory would be an explanation and transportation back to where I came from," Quist said.

"I sympathize," Elliot said. "This has been rotten bad luck for you. I gather that by now you've watched your television set and you realize just what you've gotten into."

"A kidnapping and a murder," Quist said.

"We've had bad luck, too," Elliot said. "Murder was not meant to be a part of it. You certainly were never meant to be a part of it."

"You're surely not going to tell me that if I'll be a good boy and keep my mouth shut you'll turn me loose," Quist said.

"I'm glad you understand that," Elliot said. He took a silver case from his pocket, extracted a cigarette, lit it.

"It's fairly obvious, after I've seen so many of you," Quist said.

"As I said, rotten luck for you."

"So you have come to tell me—what?" Quist said.

"You must realize that we are dealing with something very big, Mr. Quist. All the big things are working fine. Little things have got us into difficulties—a dog, a man stumbling onto a hideout, forced us to change plans in midstream. If it hadn't been for your walking into it all, it wouldn't have been necessary to move the operation from Lake Toromog to here. Once you were here, had seen this house, seen a half-dozen faces you'll never forget, the whole picture changed."

"So why did you bring me here?" Quist asked.

"You forced our hand," Elliot said. He glanced at the table where the bourbon, ice, and water carafe rested. "Mind if I make myself a drink?"

"It's your booze," Quist said.

Elliot poured himself a stiff shot on the rocks. He held up the glass, swirling the liquor around in it. "The demands for the girl's release are fairly simple on paper," he said. "X-million dollars and control of TAIF Oil. Not a giveaway, you understand. My people would buy the controlling shares, but they have to be made available. Rhaman Feydhev can make that possible. He now owns a controlling interest in the company himself."

"And control of TAIF in different hands could alter the whole energy picture and the money markets of the world," Quist said.

"In a nutshell," Elliot said. "Power is the name of the game, Mr. Quist."

"I sit here wondering," Quist said, "if the price of getting back a lost child was my castration whether I'd think it was too high." He had taken one of his thin black cigars out of his pocket. "Do you have a match? I seem to have misplaced my lighter."

Elliot produced his own lighter and held it for Quist.

"The girl is Feydhev's only child," he said.

"And you demand everything that he lives by, money, power," Quist said. "I wonder."

"I think there's very little doubt he'll pay the price," Elliot said. A frown creased his forehead.

"You're playing with chips whose value you don't really know," Quist said. "What is the daughter chip worth to Feydhev? You're going by old-fashioned, sentimental values, Elliot. 'My precious baby girl is worth the world.' How well do you know Feydhev?"

"Would you believe he has spent a weekend in this house, in this very room?"

"That doesn't tell me how well you know him," Quist said. His eyes were narrowed against the smoke from his cigar. "Will he do more than grieve if he loses his Tatiana, or will he empty his pockets, give up his world to save her? It may be he'll let her go and spend the rest of his life trying to hunt you down. Has he given you an answer yet?"

"The demands have not been made. Tomorrow."

"I hope I'm around to hear the answer," Quist said. "I have a feeling the deal may not go as smoothly as you hope. You ought to know better than I do, Elliot, what a sweet taste power has. It's a habit, a way of life, that's harder for a man like Feydhev to break than drugs or alcohol. 'Goodbye, my sweet Tatiana, but I can't give up the world I live by, the air I breathe, to save you.' Will he say that, do you think, or will he collapse and pay?"

Elliot looked unhappy.

"Interesting to look forward to," Quist said. "But more interesting, as far as I'm concerned, are your plans for me. The more you tell me, the grimmer my future looks. You won't hesitate to take a life to keep your scheme intact, will you, Elliot?"

"No, Mr. Quist. And I'm afraid there is no way on earth we can let you go."

"I've been trying to guess why you have waited so long," Quist said.

Something seemed to compel Elliot to go on talking. It was as if, somehow, talking would help to justify his actions. Listening, Quist kept his eye on Jarvis-Jones, standing by the door, gun in hand. It was a big room and Jones was a good twenty feet away. No kind of sudden move could possibly succeed. Jones's reflexes were far too good.

"Nothing has come over the television or radio yet about your disappearance from the Lake Toromog area," Elliot said. "But we have made inquiries about you, Quist. You are well enough known so that when the news breaks that you are missing it will make headlines. The question is, will it be connected in any way with the kidnapping?"

"How could it be?" Quist asked, thinking about his lighter stuffed down in the upholstery of the chair in the cabin.

"Breslin tells me they left the cabin exactly as they found it," Elliot said. "But so far, unfortunately, we've messed up on little things."

"Breslin?" Quist said.

Jones, at the doorway, laughed. "Your friend Smith," he said.

It wasn't comforting to have names revealed. It only made it more certain he was not going to get to talk to the law.

"It was so neatly arranged," Elliot said, a note of regret in his voice. "We needed an empty, isolated house in which to hold our hostage. The camps on Lake Toromog seemed ideal. People around, but the cabins out of sight. Strangers wouldn't attract any special attention. The owners of those camps have a way of lending them to friends or even renting them if they are going to be away. That's how you happened to be there, isn't it? A friend loaned you his camp?"

Quist nodded.

"We made quiet inquiries, a man who calls himself Cannikin owns one of the camps. He's a pop singer, who goes away from time to time to give concerts, make records. We made sure he'd be away for what we calculated was about the time we'd need—a week. We arranged an offer for him to perform in Philadelphia at a price he couldn't turn down. The timing was close, but perfect. He went to keep his engagement and we moved in an hour later with our hostage. No one would inquire, but if anyone did, we'd simply say we were friends of Cannikin's to whom he'd offered his camp while he was away. And then—then you appeared."

"So why didn't you tell me you were friends of Cannikin's? I wasn't trying to find out who you were. I was just trying to help an injured dog."

"One of the small things that went wrong," Elliot said. "Jarvis was a little too quick to use his gun. People might come to inquire about it. The owner of the dog might come looking for it. You had seen Jarvis, which was bad. He has a reputation with the police. Breslin and Jarvis felt they couldn't risk letting you go, talk, describe the people you'd seen. Your bad luck, Mr. Quist."

"And when I saw Miss Feydhev my number was up."

"I'm afraid so. We had to move her—and you. We had no other place prepared, so it had to be here. I keep a helicopter here and I sent my pilot to get you."

"So anyone who saw a helicopter land here last night won't think it unusual."

"Daily occurence," Elliot said. "It's my taxi to the city—and other places. So, unfortunately, you're here, a place you can easily describe. You have seen a half-dozen people you can identify, including me."

Quist's muscles ached from a growing tension.

"So what are you waiting for?" he asked.

"We don't know, yet, whether any connection will be

made between your disappearance and the kidnapping," Elliot said. "We don't see how there can be, but if there should be—"

"You think I might be worth some ransom money, too?"

"My dear Quist, any ransom anyone might pay for you wouldn't be worth the trouble, since it's painfully obvious we couldn't return you anyway. If no connection is made between your disappearance and the Feydhev case, then we simply—" He shrugged and put out his cigarette in an ashtray on the table.

"And if a connection is made?"

"Then we may need to prove to someone that you and Miss Feydhev are alive and well. If negotiators felt that you had been eliminated, they might hesitate to deal with us as quickly as they must."

"What about the girl?" Quist asked. "She has seen all of you, seen everything that I've seen."

"It will take some days, probably, for Feydhev to make the stock deal we'll demand of him," Elliot said. "The TAIF stock. He may need reassurances during that time. After that, I'm afraid Tatiana will be a danger to us that we can't afford."

"Of course you could treat her and me as you treated that black man who brought me my dinner," Quist said.

"Walter?" Elliot laughed. "You think I'm responsible for his unfortunate inability to speak? Poor fellow had cancer of the tongue and it was surgically removed. I'm no monster, Mr. Quist."

"That, I think, is a subject for debate," Quist said.

PART TWO

CHAPTER ONE

Cannikin's little cabin on the rise of ground above Pat Altman's camp was crowded with people, all talking at once, it seemed. There were Cannikin, Lydia, Garvey, a couple of troopers left behind by Stryker, suddenly joined by Kreevich, Rubek, the FBI man, Stryker, and Joe Wellman, the caretaker, who'd been nosing around outside. Kreevich had to explain to his friends that it wasn't Quist's disappearance that had brought him here. He hadn't known until fifteen minutes ago that Quist was in this part of the world, let alone missing.

Everybody had a partial theory. Kreevich had an orderly mind and he used it to separate facts from inventions. The first solid fact they had was that Cannikin's dog had been shot with the same .44 caliber handgun that had been used to murder David Peters in New York. Everything else was assumption, with no solid proof to back it up. It didn't necessarily follow that the gun had been used by the same person. Likely, but only an assumption. A lipstick-stained tissue in the bathroom wasn't proof that Tatiana Feydhev had been held here. Likely, but only an assumption. Probable, if the same person had used the .44 to murder a man and kill an injured dog.

Quist's lighter, stuffed down in the upholstery of the chair, was a fact. It was easy to assume that he had been here, that he'd left it on purpose, hoping it would be found. The evidence of a helicopter landing in the yard outside—the indentations left by the landing gear, a spot of oil—led to the assumption that desperate men had made a hasty getaway, taking Quist and the lady who'd used the tissue with them. Two facts and a handful of assumptions led to a pattern they had to accept for the moment. But where did it take them? How did you trace the flight of the helicopter? Had it gone north, south, east, west? There had been less than two hours of daylight left, if the chopper Lydia and Joe Wellman had seen was the one that had landed at Cannikin's place. Time for a lot of people to have seen it, but who pays much attention to planes or helicopters in flight these days? Common occurence. There was an army airfield forty miles away, according to Stryker. Planes and choppers flew over the lake daily and in numbers. No reason for anyone to bother to pay special attention.

"But if it landed?" Kreevich asked. "And this one did land."

"In the hills here a plane goes quickly out of sight behind elevations," Stryker said. "Choppers fly low. You could see one going down and simply imagine he was skimming some upper valley."

Information came from an unexpected source. A small boy, camping over the ridge with his parents, was excitedly interested in what was going on. He was Jerry Tinker, who had encountered Lydia the day before, who'd heard the gunshot, who'd been searching along with his elders for the missing Quist.

Jerry had gone home to carry the news to his parents after seeing Lydia. He had a CB radio and he'd switched it on to see if anyone on those channels was talking about the missing man: truck drivers, state police, some radio hams.

Young Jerry had talked to Joe Wellman outside Cannikin's cabin and Wellman had brought him in to report to Stryker and the cops from the city.

"They jabber back and forth to each other all the time," the boy said. "They got special names for each other, you know?"

Kreevich knew.

"I heard this strange one," the boy said. "It sounded like he was saying 'Oblong Courier, Oblong Courier.' Like nobody seemed to answer him. Then he came in again. 'Oblong Courier, setting down in ten minutes.' Then, 'Oblong Courier, setting down in five minutes.' Finally, he just said, 'Oblong Courier setting down.' That's all. I never heard him again."

"Did you hear a helicopter overhead?" Kreevich asked.

"Gee, Lieutenant, I couldn't swear to it. They go over all the time. This guy kept saying he was 'setting down' and I wondered if it was a plane or a chopper in trouble. But he didn't sound like he was in trouble, just passing on information."

"And nobody ever answered him?"

"I heard some guy laughing and saying, 'So set down and shut up about it.' I figured it was someone like me, tuned in by accident on this Oblong guy's channel."

Kreevich looked at Stryker. "Any way of tracing it?" he asked.

"We could put it out on the radio," the trooper sergeant said. "We might get lucky, we might not."

"Does Oblong Courier ring any bells with you, Sergeant? Some place? Some name?"

"Nothing," Stryker said.

Cannikin, the pop singer with the wind-blown hair, broke

into the conversation. "What do you know about traps, Jerry? Who would be setting traps in the woods around here? Charlie Brown got caught in one."

The boy looked uncomfortable.

"It might be helpful if you know something, son," Kreevich said. "I understand there's no hunting or trapping allowed in these woods."

"Mr. Fahnestock, down by the lake," Jerry said. "A lot of wild ducks feed just outside his place. A fox, or something, has been killing the ducks. Mr. Fahnestock set a trap for whatever it was. My father warned him he might catch something he didn't want to catch." The boy looked at Cannikin. "Charlie used to go down and check on those ducks. Never bothered them. But he must have stepped in the trap by accident."

"Bastard!" Cannikin said. He wasn't interested in murders, or kidnapping, or abductions.

"The trap didn't kill your dog," Kreevich said. "It was a man with a .44 gun."

"All I want is a chance at him," Cannikin said, "and Fahnestock ought to have his ass kicked for setting a trap."

They left the cabin in the hands of Stryker's men, searching for fingerprints. There would be a mess of them now. Kreevich walked away from the others with Lydia and Garvey.

"What do you make of it, Mark?" Garvey asked.

"Julian ran into big trouble," Kreevich said. "It looks like the people we're after. If it is, he's in really big trouble. If we can trace the flight of the chopper after it left; if the troopers come up with any fingerprints that are on record; if we can—"

"If, if, if!" Garvey said.

"One thing's certain," Kreevich said. "There's no point in you two hanging around here. Julian's a long way off by now, and he won't be back to Lake Toromog. If he has any way to get in touch, it'll be back in the city—his office, his apartment. I think that's where you ought to be."

"Mark, is there any reason for them to harm Julian?" Lydia asked, her voice unsteady.

Kreevich's face was set in grim lines. "I can't give you an honest answer, Lydia," he said. "I don't know what he saw or what he knows."

CHAPTER TWO

The chief problem the people at the Hotel Beaumont had was trying to keep an eager press corps, wandering sensation-seekers, and curious guests away from the suite on the twenty-fifth floor, occupied by Rhaman Feydhev. The newspaper, television, and radio reporters were the easiest to handle. It was made clear to them by Ray Collins, second-in-command to Frank Rubek of the FBI, that Feydhev had not yet received any communication from the kidnappers of his daughter, except for two phone calls assuring him that Tatiana was safe and unharmed. How and when the serious ransom demands would be made they didn't know. They could come over the phone, or by mail, or by messenger. Corridors must be kept clear, telephone lines open. Already, hundreds of crank calls had come to the hotel's switchboard, people with tips, people making a pretense of being the kidnappers, demanding money. Two policewomen filtered the switchboard calls. They had a routine, saying very politely that they were receiving hundreds of crank calls. To make sure they weren't talking to pretenders, please describe the clothes Miss Feydhev was wearing, the jewelry.

The facts were: a simple dark-blue taffeta dinner dress; a single ring, a topaz set in platinum; a summer fur, Alaskan sable. No one had come close so far.

Rhaman Feydhev was not a weeping, hysterical parent. A tall, dark-skinned man with a neatly trimmed Fu Manchu moustache and a small goatee, wearing a plain dark business suit, white shirt, dark tie, he sat like a statue in an armchair a few feet from the telephone manned by Agent Collins. He'd had less than a couple of hours sleep since the murder and kidnapping, but he showed no signs of fatigue. Black eyes burned brightly in dark sockets. He had smoked half-a-dozen boxes of flat Egyptian cigarettes. His secretary, an alert-looking young Englishman named Ronald James, brought him coffee and, from time to time, a glass of wine. He hadn't touched food. He had talked to no one except Agent Rubek, Agent Collins, and Sergeant Dubinsky, a homicide detective under Kreevich, who was hooked to an improvised telephone extention waiting, waiting. The few times when he left the sitting room to go to the bathroom, to take a brief nap, Ronald James went with him. As other agents and police came and went, some with questions, James did most of the talking for his employer. It was as if he had some secret telepathic contact with the millionaire, knew exactly what he was thinking, exactly what his answer would be to a question.

It was four o'clock in the afternoon of the third day. Agent Rubek hadn't appeared in the suite all day. Collins explained that the man in charge had come up with some sort of lead. When asked what kind of lead, Collins couldn't say. Or wouldn't. It seemed to make Feydhev restless.

At five minutes past four the telephone rang. Collins answered, listened a moment, and then turned to Feydhev.

"This may be it," he said.

Sergeant Dubinsky lifted his receiver. Just to the left of him a tape recorder started to turn, noiselessly. On a round table beside Feydhev's chair a squawk box had been set up so that everyone in the room could hear the conversation. Ronald James switched it on. Collins signaled to Feydhev.

"Rhaman Feydhev speaking," the millionaire said. His voice was deep, his accent British. Oxford-educated it said in Collins's file on him.

"Sorry to keep you waiting so long, Mr. Feydhev," a pleasant American voice said. "So that you will have no doubts, I was asked some questions about your daughter. She is wearing a dark-blue dinner dress, a topaz ring set in platinum, a summer fur."

"What kind of fur?" Feydhev asked.

"I'm not an expert," the American voice said, "but I think it's sable, possibly Russian."

That was enough.

"So say what you have called me to say," Feydhev said.

Everyone in the room was motionless. The little tape recorder spun without making a sound.

"I must make it quick," the American voice said, "because I know every possible preparation has been made to trace this call. It won't do you any good, by the way, when you do trace it. It's a public telephone on a street corner. The demands are quite simple, Mr. Feydhev. Twenty million dollars in cash, and a controlling interest in TAIF Oil—shares to be placed on the public market for sale to the highest bidders. The highest bidders will be my people."

"The cash is possible," Feydhev said, showing no emotion whatever. "Control of TAIF is something else again. It will take some time, several days, to make the shares you ask for available."

"We know that, Mr. Feydhev. Take however much time you need."

"Your three minutes are up," said a metallic operator's voice.

"Wait!" Feydhev said sharply.

"I'll check back with you later, operator, when I've finished my call," the American voice said.

Feydhev leaned forward in his chair. "You know the value of those TAIF shares?"

"Oh, yes, Mr. Feydhev. Their value in cash and the control and power they represent."

"Then you have to know that I must be given certain assurances from you," Feydhev said. "Put my daughter on the phone."

"Not possible. Not now. I told you, I'm calling from a street booth."

"When?"

"When you have assembled the cash, and when you are ready to put the TAIF shares on the market. And we will know whether you are working in that direction or not, Mr. Feydhev. We won't need you to tell us, we will know."

"Do you expect me to turn over a fortune to you, control of an empire, without being certain I'm getting what I pay for?"

"May I point out to you that you aren't in a position to make demands, Mr. Feydhev. We are. I'm afraid this is all the time I have for now. I'll be calling you again."

The phone clicked off. A dial tone sounded.

Feydhev brought his fist down hard on the arm of his chair.

"Sound for real, Mr. Feydhev?" Collins asked.

"Do you have any idea, Mr. Collins, what he has asked for?"

Collins smiled uneasily. "I know what twenty million dollars is. I mean, it's a figure I understand but don't quite believe."

"That is nothing," Feydhev said impatiently. "The other, the control of TAIF, that's the control of half the world!"

"The man said they would know if you were working to make that deal," Collins said. "Doesn't that suggest someone on the inside, someone in your business complex, Mr. Feydhev?"

Feydhev sat very still, staring straight ahead at the wall.

Into that moment came Agent Rubek and Lieutenant Kreevich, back from Lake Toromog. They were brought up to date on the just-ended phone call.

"Well, we have a kind of lead," Rubek said, and he told Feydhev and the others about their trip to the lake and what they'd found there.

"You think this man Quist discovered Tatiana and her captors?" Feydhev asked.

"Not much question about it," Rubek said.

"Could this Quist be part of the conspiracy, be one of them?"

"Not possibly," Kreevich said. "He's a close personal friend of mine. He doesn't need money or power."

"No man knows whether he needs power until he's had it," Feydhev said.

"Quist is now a news story," Kreevich said. "It will be connected with the murder and the kidnapping, because that's the way it is."

"Perhaps they will ask for a ransom for him, too," Feydhev said.

"We now have two people to sweat about instead of one," Kreevich said. "Your daughter wouldn't have a chance with these kinds of professionals. But Quist is a very competent, very alert, very quick-witted guy. He left that lighter for us. It put the whole picture together. If he sees any moment when he can take an action, he will."

"And get them both killed," Feydhev said, his voice flat.

He seemed to be showing the first signs of wear and tear. He lifted his heavy-lidded eyes to Kreevich. The lieutenant seemed to be the man he trusted most. Maybe it was because they were both in the same bind.

"The demands they have made on me are unthinkable," Feydhev said. "Not the money, you understand. I would pay more than twenty million for Tatiana's safe return. But the other—?"

"She's not worth that?" Kreevich asked.

"How do you place a value on one human life, even a life that is dear to you?" Feydhev asked. "Suppose I were willing to give everything I have for Tatiana? I asked the man how I could be sure I would get what I paid for. He told me I was not in a position to make demands."

"How long would it take you, using all the haste you might be expected to in this case, to arrange for this stock sale?" Kreevich asked.

"Two, three days," Feydhev said. "There are Swiss banks and American banks and even banks in Tokyo that are holding documents and securities for me. They would have to be assured that they are releasing them to me, on my orders."

"So you can buy us time," Kreevich said. "You can buy us three days, even if someone is watching you from inside your business world. You don't have to decide what you are going to do until the exact moment comes when you have to."

"What do you expect time will buy you, Lieutenant?"

"I expect to win, Mr. Feydhev. I always expect to win."

"And do you—always win?"

"No. But I try to give myself every chance," Kreevich said. "Let me point out to you what time can buy." The lieutenant's intense manner, his crisp, staccato speech, forced attention. "We have a lead. We can place your daughter and Julian Quist in a helicopter being ferried away from

Lake Toromog. Less than two hours of daylight when they took off, two hours in which someone might have paid attention in an area where planes and choppers are commonplace. An army air base close by. So we are involved in a slow, plodding inquiry on the subject. Who saw a chopper take off from Toromog? At least three people saw it come in. So far no one has reported seeing it leave. We may get lucky soon, we may not. Time is essential."

"And if someone did see it?" Feydhev asked.

"Which way was it headed? North into Vermont or New Hampshire? East into Connecticut? West into New York? South into New Jersey? Just a hint could save us from searching hundreds of thousands of square miles of territory."

Feydhev's mouth was a thin slit under his drooping moustache. "Tatiana's life depends on your finding someone with that kind of information?"

"Your daughter's life, at this moment, seems to depend on your willingness to meet the ransom demands," Kreevich said. "I get the impression, Mr. Feydhev, that you haven't decided whether you will pay or not. All I'm asking is that you go through the motions of getting ready to pay. In that time we may get lucky."

Feydhev seemed to grind his strong white teeth together. "You think I'm some kind of a heartless villain, Lieutenant? Debating whether the price for my daughter is too high?"

"If I had a daughter and she was kidnapped," Kreevich said, "when the ransom demand came, my first thought would be how to get it together. Your first thought seems to be that the price is too high."

"You don't understand—"

"Perhaps not. How much is your daughter worth on the hoof? Maybe you can make a counteroffer when the time comes. Maybe that would give us extra time, Mr. Feydhev."

"How can I be sure, if I pay, that Tatiana will be set free?

I cannot turn over to them what they ask in return for nothing. How can I be sure?" A note of desperation had crept into Feydhev's voice.

"I answered a question like that a little while ago," Kreevich said. "You can't be sure—unless you know exactly what your daughter has seen and what she knows. Your daughter has one chance that my friend Quist doesn't have. She has someone working for her on the inside."

"What are you talking about? Who?"

"Quist," Kreevich said.

CHAPTER THREE

It was a beautiful warm summer day. From the windows of his room in Elliot's house Quist looked out on a range of rolling green mountains. It had to be Vermont, he told himself. They'd only been up in the chopper another twenty minutes after he'd spotted the Bennington Monument.

Quist went close to the windows and looked down. Jarvis Jones had promised him waiting guards in the garden below. They were there. One of them walked slowly up and down under the windows, an automatic machine pistol at the ready. The other leaned back in a white garden chair, looking up. He smiled as he saw Quist framed there. Under his open jacket Quist saw the leather straps of a shoulder holster. Two men, relaxed but ready. He didn't bother to look out into the hall. He took Jones's word for the precautions.

He had managed to get about four hours of sleep, stretched out on the big canopied bed. Operating in a world that involved strange hours, late nights, stretches with no sleep at all, he had learned to take advantage of blank spots in his schedule. He could sleep on a plane, on a train, in the middle of the morning, if that was opportune. After Elliot had left him the night before, there had been nothing to do but sleep; sleep, or anguish over the impossible nature of the situation he faced. Better to sleep and be ready, at least physically, for what the next day offered. A sentence of death had been passed on him and on Tatiana Feydhev. There was, perhaps, one chance in a thousand of beating it, by some kind of physical action, which at the moment he couldn't foresee. If the chance came, he must be ready to take it.

The lock turned in the door of his room and Walter, the tongueless black man, brought in a tray. One of Elliot's gunmen was behind him in the doorway.

"The prisoner ate a hearty breakfast," Quist thought.

Orange juice, bacon and eggs, hot rolls, coffee, sweet butter, and a jar of honey. The Beaumont, the world's top luxury hotel, couldn't have done better.

"You get such a thing here as a newspaper, Walter?" he asked.

Walter made a vague gesture. They obviously got newspapers, but whether Quist would be allowed one was another matter. Quist placed the tray so that it faced the television set. He turned it on and sat down to his breakfast. Facing death, he found, had not affected a healthy appetite.

There was some kind of home show on television, an assertive blond woman discussing menus, recipes, and other culinary delights with an obvious Frenchman, whom she constantly identified as once having been the pastry chef for Princess Grace of Monaco. Quist endured it because he knew that in five minutes there would be news on the hour—eight o'clock.

He had reached a hot roll with sweet butter and honey when he discovered that he had made it. The broadcaster was full of the story of his disappearance from the camp at Lake Toromog and the certain tie-in with the murderer of David Peters and probably the kidnappers of Tatiana Feydhev. The gun that had been used to wipe out Peters had also been used to shoot a dog. There was evidence in Cannikin's cabin that both Quist and Tatiana had been there. The police had not said what evidence. There was no mention of Quist's lighter or of the tissue with lipstick on it. The police and the FBI were searching for someone who had seen a helicopter take off from the lake about six-thirty the evening before, hoping to learn what course it had taken, in what direction it had flown.

Then, suddenly, there was a friend. Lieutenant Mark Kreevich of Homicide in a sidewalk interview as he was leaving the Beaumont.

"You're sure that Julian Quist was somehow taken captive by the kidnappers, Lieutenant?" a reporter asked, holding a microphone in front of Kreevich's grim face.

"It's an assumption we have to make," Kreevich said. "Of course, Quist wasn't allowed to leave us a note, or his calling card, or his monogrammed cigarette lighter."

Quist dropped the roll he was buttering. They'd found it. They knew for certain. Good old Kreevich was letting him know, just in case he had access to news. A tiny spark of hope!"

"The FBI is handling the kidnapping aspects of the case," Kreevich was saying to the reporter. "My job is the murder of David Peters. Here we have solid evidence. The same gun was used to shoot Peters and a dog over a hundred miles away in Massachusetts. It seems fair to assume the same man handled the gun, is one of the kidnappers, and is involved in abducting Quist. My job is to find the gun and the man who carries it."

"Then, do you think—"

"Sorry. No more time for questions," Kreevich said, and his image disappeared from the screen.

"It is still not known," the broadcaster said, "whether Rhaman Feydhev has received ransom demands from the kidnappers. Agent Frank Rubek, in charge of the case for the FBI, has only a 'no comment' statement to make. It is understandable that the anxious father would have nothing to say that could lead to some crackpot fouling up his negotiations with the kidnappers."

Quist switched off the set and sipped his coffee, which had cooled. Kreevich and Rubek were very much on the trail. If someone had spotted the chopper, things might come to a head quickly. Quist wondered whether that was good or bad. Brooks Elliot had suggested that he expected negotiations to take two or three days. If they felt hurried or endangered, what would that do to his chances and Tatiana's?

A little after nine o'clock, Jarvis-Jones unlocked the door of the room, followed by Walter, who took away the breakfast tray.

"Sleep well?" Jones asked.

"Fine," Quist said.

Jones chuckled. "Nerves of steel, eh? The boss has a little business to transact with you downstairs." From his pocket he produced the handcuffs. "Just so you don't get it in your head to make a run for it," he said.

It took both Jones's hands to fasten one loop of the cuffs to Quist's right wrist, the other to his own left. The gun was in the holster under his jacket. Quist curbed a wild impulse to make his move now. But there was a man in the hall, men in the garden, others stationed in places he didn't know about. The moment would be like this, he told himself, but not now; not till he knew more about the geography of the house and grounds. He looked at Jones with new eyes. He had known him as the casual shooter of an injured dog, a member of the kidnap gang, but now, from the latest TV report, he knew that Jones had shot David Peters in cold blood. Same gun, same man—quick triggered, unfeeling.

"We're getting to be like Siamese twins," Jones said. "But don't get the notion I feel any brotherly love for you, Quist. You really screwed things up for us."

"Oh, I wouldn't say that," Quist said. "You're the one who had to shoot the dog and attract attention. If you'd just kept your nose indoors, I'd have freed the dog from the trap and gone about my business. If I were running the show, I'd present you with a bill for expenses against your share of the ransom. You're a clumsy fellow, Jarvis."

Jarvis-Jones gave a sharp little tug on the handcuff. "Wise guy," he said. "Downstairs."

They walked down the graceful staircase into the entrance hall Quist had seen the night before. Off to one side was a door leading into a handsomely appointed library—walls of books, a big, flat-top reading table with Colonial armchairs set around it, an overstuffed couch, and several leather-covered armchairs, all with their own special reading lamps.

Brooks Elliot, Smith—or Breslin—were there, along with two of their armed guards, whose faces Quist photographed in his mind. Across the room, looking small and frightened, was Tatiana Feydhev. She seemed to brighten a little at the sight of Quist. He smiled at her.

"Good morning, Mr. Quist," Elliot said. "No need for the handcuffs here, Jarvis."

Jarvis used his key to unlock the cuffs.

Freed, Quist reached into his pocket for one of his cigars. Elliot smiled at him and tossed him a book of matches. "I remember you told me last night you've lost your lighter, Quist. I wonder if you left it in Cannikin's cabin."

"I don't know where I lost it," Quist said. "Maybe there, maybe in the woods."

"Oh, Breslin remembers that you had it in the cabin," Elliot said. "I wondered if that homicide detective on TV was trying to send you a message."

Don't underestimate this man, Quist thought.

"We need some cooperation from you and Miss Feydhev," Elliot said.

Quist lit a cigar and pocketed the book of matches. "Which we are supposed to give you cheerfully?"

" 'While there is life—' " Elliot said. "In spite of what I told you very frankly last night, you must still be hoping, Mr. Quist. I saw the way you looked at Jarvis when he bent down to unfasten the cuffs. You were looking at the side of his neck almost clinically, my friend. One good karate chop and off to the races. Isn't that what you were thinking?" His amiable smile widened. "No chance at all, Quist. Our security isn't limited to Jarvis or to those of us you see in this room. If you try heroics you will only be costing yourself a little time."

Among other things, Elliot was something of a mind reader.

"Now to the business at hand," Elliot said. "We have made our demands on Rhaman Feydhev for his daughter's release. He, not unnaturally, asks to be reassured that his daughter is alive and well. And you, Mr. Quist."

"Why me?"

"They have concluded that we have you. If you, too, are alive and well, they would be able to hope that we aren't—what was the word we used last night, Mr. Quist—monsters? We can't do what Feydhev wants. We can't put his daughter on the phone, or you. The whole damn FBI is set up to trace calls. So we have decided to let each of you tape a message. Just a few sentences in your own style. We can, of course, edit the tape or have you make another one."

"I could tell you to go shove it," Quist said.

Elliot nodded patiently. "But the girl still believes she has a future, Quist. It would be cruel to disillusion her while she still has some time, don't you think? If you refuse, it might cause her needless anxiety." He gestured to Breslin, who produced a cassette tape recorder from the drawer of the reading table. "Just address your remarks 'to whom it may concern,' Quist."

Quist was thinking harder than he ever could remember: a way to communicate something to the FBI and Kreevich that wouldn't be instantly obvious.

"All ready, Quist," Breslin-Smith said. He held out a small recording microphone.

Quist took it, fighting to keep his hand from shaking. He took a deep breath. "To whom it may concern," he said into the microphone, "this is Julian Quist, and you must know that I am a prisoner of Miss Feydhev's kidnappers. This is a bruiser, but I'm not hurt, and I've been treated extraordinarily well. Please urge Feydhev to get on with meeting the ransom demands. Miss Feydhev and I both want out! Lydia, I love you."

He handed the microphone back to Breslin-Smith. "I suppose you'll edit out that last," he said.

"I don't think so," Elliot said. "A rather nice human touch, I think." He turned to Tatiana, a man searching for words. Then he spoke, haltingly, in the language that Quist couldn't identify. Breslin held out the microphone to the girl. She hesitated, and then she almost rushed to take it.

Words poured out of her, emotional, high pitched. There were tears in the sound of her voice. She was pleading. It went on for a couple of minutes, and then she lowered her head and held out the microphone to Breslin.

"Impressive, I think," Elliot said. "We'll have to go over the translation before we send it, but as I could follow it, I think it's just what we wanted."

"Papa's heart should melt, from the sound of it," Quist said.

"Now, Mr. Quist," Elliot said. "I'm going to ask you to share this room with Miss Feydhev for the rest of the day. It will save us from employing two sets of watchdogs. You'll find plenty to read. I'll have a portable TV set brought in, if you like, so you can see and hear what your friends are doing. The windows are locked, but the room is air-conditioned. There is a lavatory opening off the far end there. Walter will provide you with food and drink at intervals. Is there anything I've overlooked?"

"Just ten minutes alone with you without your goons," Quist said.

"I appreciate how much you would like that," Elliot said. "I'm afraid I can't afford the time. If I could, I might surprise you, Mr. Quist."

He gave a signal, and Breslin, carrying the tape recorder, Jarvis-Jones, and the two bodyguards left the room with them. The door lock turned. Quist was alone with Tatiana. She looked at him, and he was struck again by a kind of tragic beauty.

"They're not going to let us go, are they?" she said, in perfect English, without a trace of accent except for a slight British coloring.

CHAPTER FOUR

A race against time, Kreevich thought. Two days, three at the outside, in which to find answers to loose ends that just might head them in the right direction before it was too late.

Kreevich's entire adult life had been involved with crime and criminals. He had learned to think like the criminals he was hunting might think. Lydia had asked him for some hopeful comment about Quist's chances. Feydhev had put the same kind of question to him about his daughter. "It depends on what they've seen and what they know," he'd answered to both questions. If either Lydia or Feydhev chose to take hope from that answer, so be it. Kreevich felt very little optimism, himself, about the outcome of this affair for his friend Quist or the millionaire's daughter. Part of the kidnappers' demands was simple enough to understand—the huge cash payment. In an ordinary kidnapping, money was the primary object. You delivered it in unmarked, untraceable bills, and the kidnappers evaporated with it and spent their futures in luxury. The kidnap victim might or might not be able to identify some faces, but those faces would disappear into the huge population of the world, to faraway places, where appearances could easily be changed. A beard where there had been none, a clean-shaven face where there had been a beard. An identification, based on a police artist's drawing from the victim's description, could be an utterly futile lead. In such a case, the kidnappers could set their victim free without too much risk.

There was, however, a second part to the demands made on Feydhev that Kreevich hadn't yet grasped in all its complexity. The turnover of TAIF Oil stock, and with it the transfer of power, was something that Kreevich didn't yet understand. When someone else owned control, wasn't that person instantly identified as part of the kidnap conspiracy? How could the exchange of power be made without its being a confession?

Given an answer to those questions, you looked at something so enormous in value that one or two lives were an insignificant price to pay to make certain nothing went wrong.

The picture of what had happened outside the Beaumont

the night of the abduction was cloudy. Waters, the doorman, had been missing from his post. One taxi driver, in his rear-view mirror, had seen Tatiana Feydhev "wrestled" into a dark-colored car. Were the men who seized her masked? Ski masks had become a popular cover in the last ten years of violence in a violent world. The taxi driver had been uncertain, even when it was suggested to him. The men, he thought, wore hats. It was dark. The second taxi driver, who ducked when he heard shots, saw nothing. He heard a car racing away, but he didn't risk looking at it. The man walking his dog across the avenue had heard the shots, turned, seen the fallen David Peters on the sidewalk. A man with a gun was running toward a car that took off. He wore a hat. The dog walker didn't get a very good look at him, saw no face, didn't think at the time of a mask. His main concern was with the man he was sure had been shot dead. No other witnesses had come forward from anywhere. The whole thing hadn't taken more than a minute to a minute and a half.

This led to other questions, which Kreevich had asked himself over and over. The whole thing was so carefully planned that Cannikin's cabin on Lake Toromog, a hundred and twenty miles from the city, must have been part of it. Questions: Had they driven Tatiana Feydhev all the way to the lake in that black, blue, or green car that might have been a Chevy Nova? Had they switched cars somewhere on the way? Having arrived at Cannikin's cabin—they must have known he would be gone for a week—what did they do with the car? They had taken off in a helicopter. Had the car been left behind somewhere? Sergeant Stryker of the State Police hadn't been able to locate an unaccounted-for car. Kreevich had to think the driver had taken the car away after delivering Tatiana and her captors. The original plan, spoiled somehow by Quist's appearance, must have been to return for them later in the week. One more question kept gnawing at Kreevich. Cannikin had not played it like a man involved. His grief over the shooting of his dog had seemed genuine. He'd led Stryker to proof that someone had occupied the cabin in his absence. But it was his cabin and his absence had to have been timed exactly to match the kidnappers' plan. Could the pop singer know something more than he had told them?

Stryker had not come up with anything helpful about the departure of a helicopter from the lake the evening of Quist's disappearance. The people there were so accustomed to planes and choppers being overhead that none had taken any particular notice, it seemed. Several people who carried CB radios in their cars or trucks had heard the same signal that Jerry Tinker had intercepted: Oblong Courier. None of them had heard it before. They had all assumed they'd somehow gotten onto a channel used by the Army Air Force base. Oblong Courier must be the name of a plane, or perhaps a tactical exercise. The communications officer at the base reported that Oblong Courier meant nothing to him. There was no plane or exercise using that designation flying out of the base.

No lead to anything.

After checking out with Stryker by phone, Kreevich returned to Feydhev's suite in the Beaumont. His question about TAIF had to be answered. Feydhev, through young Mr. James, his secretary, begged to be excused. He was involved in a series of overseas calls. Kreevich had asked him to set things in motion, hadn't he?

"Are you indispensable to him at the moment, Mr. James?" Kreevich asked.

"No one is indispensable to Mr. Feydhev," James said. His smile was pleasant, boyish. He had wavy brown hair, carefully styled, brown eyes that seemed to have no deception in them. He looked like a nice college kid, Kreevich thought.

"I need help to make sense out of some of this," Kreevich said.

"Don't we all," James said. His British speech was attractive.

"The TAIF part of the kidnappers' demands doesn't make sense to me," Kreevich said.

"It's hard to conceive of how much wealth and power it involves," James said.

They sat down on either end of the living room couch from each other. Kreevich, a cigarette chain-smoker, was squinting at the young secretary through a cloud.

"How can the kidnappers make use of what they get without revealing themselves?" Kreevich asked.

"My first thought when I heard the demands," James said. "Mr. Feydhev has made it reasonably clear to me."

"Try it on me for size," Kreevich said.

"Mr. Feydhev's stock in TAIF would be put on the market, sold to the highest bidders, according to the demands. The price of that stock would skyrocket, but it is worth almost any price if a controlling block can be bought. The buyers, Mr. Feydhev thinks, will come from his part of the world, the Middle East: the oil sheiks, who have most of the world by the short hairs these days. He thinks it will be a group, not one man, eager to take over from him—his business enemies."

"So they reveal themselves, unmask themselves."

"I'm sure it's occurred to you, Lieutenant, that the actual kidnappers of Tatiana and your friend Quist are professionals. You can buy these professionals in violence today anywhere from Tokyo to Warsaw. These men are probably being paid a handsome fee for their services, perhaps the twenty million dollars extracted from Mr. Feydhev. But TAIF will go to the men who are really behind it, a group of men. They will buy the shares on the open market, innocent as you please. You will never in the world be able to connect them with the actual kidnappers. Mr. Feydhev may guess, may think he knows when the time comes, but proof will be something else. It may well be that some of the buyers will have no idea why Mr. Feydhev put his stock on the market."

"If they can read or listen to the radio or watch television they'll know," Kreevich said.

"But they won't back away from the opportunity to take control of TAIF just because Mr. Feydhev has had his arm twisted. They will not be committing a crime by buying his shares. They're on the market, they'll bid for them."

"So, whatever happens, Mr. Feydhev will get back his twenty million dollars, probably more, through the sale of his stock."

Young Mr. James smiled and shook his head. "The money is a very small part of it, Lieutenant. It may sound like telephone numbers to you and me, but it's not that important to Mr. Feydhev. What matters to him is that he is stripped of power by a vicious and violent blackmail. If it should happen, God knows what he will do to get even. He's not a forgiving man, Lieutenant."

"You say 'if it should happen.' You think when it comes down to the wire he may not think his daughter is worth the price?"

"That would mean your friend, too," James said. "What I think, Lieutenant, is that he would spend twenty million to rescue her, or twice that. I think if you could locate her he would hire his own professionals, one army to wipe out another. But whether he will hand over TAIF? I can't make an educated guess on that just yet."

Kreevich lit a fresh cigarette. "The voice on the phone suggested that someone on the inside would let them know if he was making a genuine move to sell his stock in TAIF. Any ideas?"

James smiled. "I thought you might be wondering about me," he said.

"It occurred to me," Kreevich said.

"The conspirators are overlooking one thing," James said. "For the next two or three days Mr. Feydhev will do everything necessary to make his stock in TAIF available for sale. It will be for real, not a fake. All anybody could report to the conspirators is that it's in the works. But when the moment comes, the moment to unload, then Mr. Feydhev will make the decision that counts. Yes or no."

"How much does he love his daughter?"

"How does one measure that?" James asked, "By heartbeats? By dollars? By power? I just can't give you an answer, Lieutenant. Let me suggest one thing. He's trying to buy the time you asked for. I think he prays, in his own way, for your success. But if you fail, I can't predict what the next step will be."

"You're saying Fehdhev may not be willing to go all the way to free his child."

"Lieutenant Kreevich, there is a great deal of talk these days in big power structures about how to deal with modern terrorism. We see it over and over, hostages taken, demands made to release political prisoners, transportation of those prisoners to some place safe for them. The heads of governments, the people in power, have to have a policy. If you give in today, new demands will be made tomorrow, new hostages taken, new bomb threats carried out. Some governments have decided not to yield to this kind of pressure. Look what the Israelis did at Entebbe. They refused the demands made on them and then staged a magnificent and heroic rescue. They did the best they could for their people, all they could without giving in. I think Mr. Feydhev's attitude may parallel the Israelis. He does not want to give in to the demands of the kidnappers, perhaps he will not. But I know he would risk money, lives, even his own life, to rescue his daughter."

"Unlike the Jewish leaders at Entebbe," Kreevich said, "we don't know where the hostages are being held. An army is useless if you can't locate the enemy."

CHAPTER FIVE

Quist stared at the girl across the room, looking, he imagined, like the village idiot. All the time in the cottage at the lake, all the time during the trip in the chopper, when she had clung so desperately to him, all during this just-finished exchange with Elliot, this had been a one-language girl, English beyond her. Now she spoke it as if it were her primary tongue.

"Would you like to explain all the sign language and the gobbledegook? I mean, for God sake, Tatiana—"

"You've got it right now, my name," she said.

"Television."

"Ah, yes. I had a crazy idea—Julian is it? Julian Quist. I like it."

"Just explain the language thing before your English leaves you," Quist said.

She gave him a very American little grin. "It won't leave me, Julian. Would you believe I've spent a lot of my life dreaming about what I'd do if ever I was kidnapped? After all, my father is one of the richest men in the world."

"Not a fantasy many of us indulge in, I imagine."

"I decided I would play the role of a terrified Arab girl,

speaking my native dialect only. That way the kidnappers might get careless in my presence and I could overhear something that would be useful to me. Since I speak five languages fluently, it seemed like a good idea. Incidentally, you need a little brushing up on your French. Intelligible, but a really ghastly accent, Julian."

"So what did you hope to hear?"

"Their plans, where we were exactly, anything I could use."

"Use to do what?"

"Escape," she said. She shrugged her shoulders in a casual way. "You see, I think you should know, Julian, that my father will never buy my freedom. He will negotiate as long as they will let him, but in the end he won't pay."

"That's your assessment of him?"

"No," she said gravely. "He has told me that. Warned me."

"And yet, knowing you could be a target, he let you run around the city without any security precautions?"

"It may be hard for you to understand, Julian, because you haven't lived in my kind of world. My father is an unbelievably rich and unbelievably powerful man. Clever people would never bother me because they would know that in the end my father would catch up with them. I had only to watch out for idiots. Would I spend my life locked up in a cage somewhere, just to be safe? I would rather be dead than live locked away."

"I don't think we've fallen into the hands of idiots."

She laughed and tossed back a stray lock of her dark hair. "I look at this creature, Elliot, and at Smith and Jones and the others, and I want to tell them what fools they are. In the not-too-distant future they will all be dead. My father will see to that."

"And you and I?" he asked quietly.

"You and I," she said confidently, "will find a way."

A gutsy girl, Quist thought, but not very practical. She had fantasied being a heroine in such a situation all her life, but she seemed a little short on method.

"Our Mr. Elliot gave me a hint as to what the demands are that are being made on your father," Quist said. "A few million dollars and control of TAIF Oil."

"Oh, my!" Tatiana said, her mobile face gone somber. "There would be more chance of my father's delivering if they'd asked for the moon. TAIF is the center of his life."

"He's apparently talking," Quist said. "That's the reason for all this taping here this morning."

"He will talk as long as they will let him, hoping he can locate me and come after me, hoping that I may find some way out myself. But he will never turn over TAIF Oil."

"So, like the weather, we can talk about it, but there is nothing we can do about it."

Her eyes were very bright. "We can make it hard for them when the time comes. Were you thinking about a karate chop to Mr. Jones neck?"

"Something like that."

"I'm very good at that sort of thing, when the time comes," Tatiana said. "One thing my father insisted on was that I learn how to protect myself."

Half a dozen men with guns; one, at least, with a machine pistol. Not good gambling odds.

"What happened to your karate skills the night you were abducted?" he asked.

She dropped down in a chair by the windows, turned away from him. In profile she was lovely, almost as lovely as Lydia.

"I was always told by my instructors, 'Think only of yourself,' " she said. "I let myself be concerned for David, and I lost my chance. Poor David."

"Jones shot him?"

She nodded. "Once between the eyes, once in the heart. He's terribly good with that gun."

"I saw him use it on Cannikin's dog. I wasn't encouraged to take chances with him."

"When we got out of the taxi in front of the hotel there were suddenly three men," Tatiana said. "Jones, the man named Breslin, or Smith, and a third man. Breslin and the third man each grabbed me by an arm and started to drag me toward a parked car. Jones was looking for interference from anywhere. I understand now the doorman had been lured away. I had a chance then to break away and run for the safety of the hotel. I think I might have made it, but I saw David moving on Jones and I shouted at him not to. In that moment someone struck me over the head from behind. I think it was the driver of the car. It wasn't enough to knock me out, but enough to keep me from using any skills I have. I saw Jones shoot, I saw David go down. It was awful, Julian." She took a deep breath. "Then I was in the car and we were racing away, Breslin and the third man almost literally sitting on me. Jones was in front with the driver, turned my way, playing with his gun. Breslin told me if I kept still, didn't try to attract attention, I'd be all right. If I didn't obey, Jones would finish me with his gun and they'd roll me out into the gutter. I looked at Jones and I believed him."

"They drove you straight to Lake Toromog?"

"I was a little foggy at first," she said. "They seemed to be driving in and out of side streets, as if they thought someone might be following. Then I heard the driver say there wasn't anyone; they were in the clear. Then we seemed to straighten away to steady driving. I don't know the city, Julian, or the highways. But there were two toll bridges, or at least toll-paying barriers. Each time I thought I might attract attention, but Jones was ready. You pay by dropping coins in a metal basket. There seemed to be no one about. It was dark, very dark except for street lights. I read a sign: Saw Mill River Parkway. Later I saw 'Brewster,' then 'Pawling.' All this in the first hour. Later 'Kent.' Then a larger town with shops and banks, all closed up, 'Great Barrington.' "

"You took a tour of three states—New York, Connecticut, Massachusetts," Quist said. "Lake Toromog is only a few miles from Great Barrington."

"They seemed to know exactly where they were going," Tatiana said. "Right after Great Barrington they turned off what seemed to be a main highway onto back roads. There were houses, but few lights. Everyone in that part of the world seemed to be asleep."

"Must have been going on three in the morning," Quist said, "considering the distance you covered."

"The man Breslin kept warning the driver not to exceed the speed limit. They didn't want to be picked up."

"I can imagine. By then there must have been alarms out all over the area. What else did they talk about, Tatiana?"

"At first they just asked me if I was all right, whether I wanted to change my position. Would I care for coffee? They had some in a Thermos." She smiled. "I kept babbling at them in Arabic. They finally got the idea that I didn't speak English."

"Your childhood scheme was working."

"But it didn't do me much good; hasn't done me much good so far," Tatiana said. "In the car, Breslin got the idea. 'We'll need the boss to translate for this doll,' he said. Jones was looking at me in a way that didn't make me happy, Julian. I've had men look at me in that sexual way before. 'Who cares what she has to say?' he said."

"The 'boss' is obviously this man Elliot," Quist said. "Did they say anything more about him, or mention this place?"

"No. We reached the camp in the woods. It was dark, deserted. Jones got out of the car and scouted around. He always had that gun. He evidently found a way in at the back, came through the cabin, turning on lights, and opened the front door. 'All clear,' he said. Then Breslin spoke to the driver. He called him 'Jack.' He was to call 'the boss' when he found an isolated phone booth and tell him everything had gone 'according to Hoyle.' He said, 'I don't want to use the radio except in an emergency.' "

"They took you into the cabin then?"

She nodded. "The third man took off with the driver, leaving just Breslin and Jones. Breslin made coffee and some sandwiches in the kitchen. Jones just sat there, smiling at me, his gun ready. Animal! I knew what he was thinking."

"But no move at you?"

"No. Except—when he passed close to me in the comings and goings, he would manage to touch me: my cheek, my hair, my shoulder. The idiot thought I must be swooning with eagerness for the right moment to come. But he and Breslin took turns catnapping, one of them dozing, one of them watching me. Then it was daylight, then morning. Breslin made breakfast, eggs and toast and coffee."

"They didn't talk about their plans?"

"No. Just sitting and waiting seemed to be it. I imagined the 'boss' had already contacted my father and they were simply waiting for the results. There was nothing—except Jones leering at me—until well into the afternoon. Then we heard the dog, snarling and crying out. Breslin was upset. Someone would hear it and come snooping around. The dog kept coming closer and closer till he sounded right outside the cabin. 'I'll shut him up,' Jones said. He went out, there was the shot, and then—there you were, Julian. After that you know as much as I do. Breslin started to use the radio he had in a back room. He felt they had to move—to bring us here."

"I kept you from a quiet vacation at beautiful Lake Toromog," Quist said. His laugh was humorless. "Well, my dear Tatiana, what the hell do we do now? Your father isn't going to pay the ransom, and even if he did, Elliot has no intention of letting us go free so that we can identify him, his men, and this place."

"Do we know where this place is?" she asked.

"Eight, ten miles from the Bennington Monument in Bennington, Vermont," Quist said. "We weren't flying for more than twenty minutes at the outside when we passed over the monument."

The girl turned in her chair. Somehow Quist had the absurd feeling that he had always known her, that she was an old, close friend.

"One thing that puzzles me, Julian," she said, "about this house. It doesn't seem like a temporary hideout. Everything runs so smoothly: the service from the kitchen, the clean towels in the bathroom, the hangar for the helicopter. You noticed it?"

Quist nodded. "Elliot told me he used the copter as a taxi to take him back and forth to the city. No one would pay any attention to it, he said."

"So Elliot has to be well known by the people who live in this area," Tatiana said. "Residents, tradespeople, the telephone and electric light companies. What happens if some neighbor walks in and sees Breslin, Jones, half a dozen other gunmen? What about the servants who work in the kitchen, who keep the house clean? It's a spotless house, you know. How long can they all stay undercover without making someone suspicious?"

"I'm afraid, Tatiana, they don't expect to be staying here long. Unless we can find a way to make a move, and in a hurry, I don't think it's going to matter much to us what the neighbors think."

CHAPTER SIX

The offices of Julian Quist Associates, high above Grand Central Station in New York, were always a swirl of activity. Clients came and went, a telephone switchboard was always loaded with calls. Temperamental actors, actresses, and other public figures staged magnificent entrances and exits. Through all this daily hubbub a cool, efficient staff handled things without confusion, protected the top brass where protection was needed.

The first bastion of defense was Miss Gloria Chard in the reception room, sitting in the center of a circular desk, surrounded by telephones. Glorious Chard, Dan Garvey had dubbed her long ago. Messenger boys delivered luncheons to the wrong office just to get a look at her. The mailman always seemed to have something for Gloria to sign, and he would lean over her while she did it, breathing as if on his way up the elevator hadn't been running. Gloria enjoyed every minute of it, but whatever her sex life was, it was handled discreetly and in secret. Garvey was considered the best bet by the stenographic pool, but no one knew for certain.

This morning, however, the atmosphere was unusual in the offices of Julian Quist Associates. Gloria Chard's reception room was crowded with people, some of them clients, some reporters, some just curious people from the building, or even off the sidewalks far below. The news was out. Julian Quist was missing, apparently abducted by the people who had murdered David Peters and kidnapped Tatiana Feydhev.

Robert Sebastian, the glamorous British actor who was starring in a smash hit on Broadway, was not concerned with his own image that morning. He was concerned for a friend, the man who had helped to make him famous. He set the tone for other clients who had come to ask for news. Was it true? Was there any news? Was there anything they could possibly do to help?

Gloria Chard, who normally delighted in handling demanding people, was not quite herself. Like everyone else in the office, she was shaken by what she'd heard over her breakfast coffee. The day before, Garvey had raced out of the office saying that Julian was lost in the woods at Lake Toromog. Gloria wasn't too concerned. Julian would never stay lost, would find his way out, would communicate when he could. She knew there were no phones in the cabins at the lake. Julian had made that clear when he left for his holiday. There would be no way to reach him, to lure him back. Now they knew he was in the hands of a killer.

Gloria had nothing to tell any of the anxious people in her reception room that they hadn't already heard on TV or radio, or read in the early afternoon edition of the *Post.* It went on like that most of the day. If there was any hopeful news it would be delivered here.

In the late afternoon there was a buzz of excitement. Reporters knew the man who walked briskly into the reception room from the outer hall. He was Lieutenant Mark Kreevich of Manhattan Homicide. They tried to block his passage, but Kreevich fed them a "no comment," gestured a greeting to Gloria, and went down the hall to the private offices.

Quist's private sanctum, with its chromium-trimmed modern furniture, the modern paintings on the walls, the portable bar, was a familiar place to Kreevich. The faces he saw there were not. There was Garvey, grim and weary from lack of sleep; Bobby Hilliard, who looked like a happy-go-lucky young Jimmy Stewart under normal conditions, seemed stunned. Connie Parmalee, a tall girl with coppery red hair, grey-green eyes behind tinted, wire-rimmed granny glasses, was Quist's secretary. She was, Kreevich knew, one of those treasures who anticipated her employer's every need, was already ahead of him when he asked for something. She was, Kreevich also guessed, like many others like her, in love with the man she worked for. If it hadn't been for Lydia Morton, this tall girl with the lovely legs might have had a dream come true. These people today were not the bright, happy, competent crew Kreevich knew so well. The sky had fallen in on them, and they didn't know how to function.

Kreevich looked around. "Lydia?" he asked.

"She's at Julian's apartment," Garvey said. "Just in case some word might come there."

Kreevich answered the question they all asked simply by their tensions.

"Nothing very concrete, but we've heard, indirectly, from Julian."

"Heard!" It was a chorus.

Feydhev, Kreevich explained, had been in touch with the kidnappers by phone. He had demanded assurances, mainly that he be allowed to talk to his daughter and to Quist.

"They keep calling from street phones in different parts of the city," Kreevich said. "Obviously they can't trot their prisoners out into the middle of Madison Avenue traffic. In any case, I think they're probably hundreds of miles away."

"The caller here, the real action somewhere else?" Garvey asked.

"Yes. They reached a compromise with Feydhev, however. They would make a recording of his daughter's voice—and Julian's. About an hour ago, some seven hours after the compromise was reached, Feydhev got word that the tape was in a phone booth in the lobby of his own hotel, the Beaumont. It was there, we have played it, made copies of it. I've brought one for you to hear. You have a cassette machine, don't you, Connie?"

The secretary went quickly into her own office and returned with a tape player.

"The girl's message is in Arabic," Kreevich said. "They're making a translation of it, but it seemed to satisfy Feydhev. Julian's little message comes first." He handed Connie the cassette and she fitted it into the machine. It started to turn, and then Julian, sounding alive, cheerful, came on:

> To whom it may concern: This is Julian Quist, and you must know that I am a prisoner of Miss Feydhev's kidnappers. This is a bruiser, but I'm not hurt, and I've been treated extraordinarily well. Please urge Feydhev to get on with meeting the ransom demands. Miss Feydhev and I both want out! Lydia, I love you.

"He doesn't sound beat up!" Bobby Hilliard said.

Connie Parmalee had turned away, fighting tears, an unheard-of thing for her.

"Lydia should hear it," Garvey said.

"I didn't bring this over to play for you just to cheer you up," Kreevich said. "You know Julian left his lighter in that cabin for us to find. I know him, and I know that no matter how tough the situation is, he'll try to get some kind of word to us if he can. I looked for something in what he says on the tape but nothing came through to me. You people who are closer to him—?"

"Play it again, Connie," Garvey said.

They listened, and then sat looking at each other.

"A little too jaunty for the situation," Bobby Hilliard said. "I'd have expected a straighter kind of plea for help."

"Keep your spirits up, all that kind of jive," Garvey said.

"I think Lydia should hear it," Connie said, back in control. "He mentions her specially. Maybe she'll hear something in it we don't."

"He mentions her specially because he loves her," Garvey said.

"Thanks for reminding me," Connie said. She was already dialing the number at Quist's apartment.

Lydia answered on the first ring. She listened as they played the tape for her, her excitement fading. She saw nothing in the message. She cherished the words at the end but, to her, they meant only just what they said.

"There was just one thing about it, after I'd listened three or four times," Kreevich said. "I've known Julian for a long time. I'm familiar with his way of talking, the slang he uses. I don't think I ever heard him call anything a 'bruiser.' It conveys a meaning—a rough situation—but I don't think I ever heard Julian use the word."

"Maybe he thought I'd appreciate it," Garvey said, still hunting for something more significant in the message. "It was a kind of an in-house joke when I first joined the firm some years ago."

"So what's the joke?" Kreevich asked.

"When we first promoted the arena out on the Island there were regular fight nights," Garvey said. "Every Friday, all winter. There was a fighter who must have been a favorite of the matchmaker out there, a heavyweight who fought more than most. His name was Bruiser Elliot. He couldn't box worth a damn, but he would maul, and punch, and lean on his man until he wore him down. A big clumsy bruiser. When he got on you he was tough. For a while there, whenever we came up with a rough problem here in the office we'd call it a bruiser—after Bruiser Elliot. Nothing more than that, and Julian's certainly got a rough problem. We stopped using it long ago. Bruiser got his brains knocked out and the phrase wasn't current anymore. But I suppose, in a tight spot, Julian thought it would mean something to me."

"And does it?" Kreevich asked.

"Only what I've just said."

"What ever became of Bruiser Elliot?" Kreevich asked.

Garvey shrugged. "Last I heard he was playing bit parts in Hollywood—movies, TV. With what's left of his face he could play monsters in horror films without any makeup."

"He could be checked." Kreevich said.

Garvey laughed. "You think Julian was trying to tell us something about Bruiser? Never. Bruiser couldn't add up to ten, let alone twenty million. And when it comes to controlling oil empires!"

"He could be a strong-arm boy for somebody," Kreevich said. "Julian may have found himself being guarded by someone he knew. Trying to tell us just that."

"You're reaching, Lieutenant."

"It might be easy to check on Bruiser Elliot," Connie said. "Screen Actors Guild should know if he'd worked for someone out there."

"See if you can come up with anything, Connie," Kreevich said.

Connie went into her own office to make phone calls. Garvey switched on the machine and they listened to the tape once more. Eventually Connie came back into the room.

"You can forget about Bruiser Elliot," she said. "He was making a Western on location, somewhere in Utah. He was thrown off a horse and he's been in a hospital out there, in traction, for the last three weeks."

"Well, that's that," Kreevich said. "Were there any special tricks this guy Elliot used in the ring, Dan? Any special gimmicks that might suggest something to us?"

"The Bruiser was just a brawler," Garvey said.

"Well, maybe a brawl would help Julian at the moment," Kreevich said, "but we have to find him to start one. I thought maybe there was something on the tape. Probably wrong."

It was after five. Anxious friends in the outer offices were told there was nothing to report. Staff people went their separate ways, probably intending to stay glued to a TV set somewhere. Only Connie Parmalee remained behind. She would sleep on a cot in her office, her phone connected to an open line from the switchboard. If, by any chance, Julian could get to a phone—

Dan Garvey walked across town to Quist's apartment on Beekman Place. It was a bad time for all of them, but particularly for Lydia. Their business, their loyalties, their friendships were all tied into Julian, but with Lydia it involved an intimacy, a special kind of sharing. People who saw them together, Lydia and Julian, must have been impressed with a kind of exotic style—he looking as if his profile had been lifted from an antique Greek coin, she a glowing, confident, electric woman. There was a little lacquer on the surface, Garvey thought, special attention paid to a carefully cultivated image that went with their special world. But Garvey knew them in their private world, their private living, and he knew there wasn't a shred of pretense to that. Julian and Lydia were more married than a dozen marriages put together. Garvey had never heard a word of backbiting, any kind of public put-down, any disagreement. They seemed to sense each others needs and wants. Garvey had seen Quist leave parties he was enjoying without a word coming from Lydia. He knew that she had some reason to want to go, and he didn't ask what it was or protest. In reverse he had seen Lydia hang in long after her pleasure was over if Quist was having a ball. They seemed to know when to give and when to take. "One plus one equals one," Garvey had said about them. He had been looking for a Lydia for himself for a long time, without any luck. She was one of a kind, he was convinced.

Julian would want her cared for and so Garvey went to

her. She answered his ring at the doorbell almost before he took his finger off the button.

"Oh, Dan, thanks for coming," she said. "Zimmer phoned me you were on the way up."

Zimmer was the doorman in the apartment building. He had asked Garvey, anxiously, about Julian downstairs. The whole world knew what had happened.

They went out on the terrace of the duplex apartment, which overlooked the East River. Without asking, Lydia produced an Irish whiskey highball for Garvey. They sat down in comfortable wicker chairs, watching a barge moving slowly down the river in the twilight.

"Nothing for you?" Garvey asked. He needed the drink.

"I keep feeling that suddenly there'll be something to do," she said. "If I started I would probably bomb out."

"I've never seen you tight in all the time I've known you," he said.

"You've never seen me in a situation where I had the impulse," she said. "My God, Dan, you have no idea what it's like to do nothing, not know anything to do."

"We're all in the same boat," Garvey said. "That goes for Mark Kreevich, too. And the FBI, from what he tells me."

"The tape? I didn't find anything special about it, except that Julian had to be alive to make it."

"Thank God for that."

"Mark thought Julian might have tried to convey some kind of message to us. He hit on the words Julian used—'This is a bruiser.' I told him it used to be a sort of office gag for a while. You remember Bruiser Elliot?"

"The fighter? Yes. He wasn't very good as I recall, just tough."

"Mark thought Julian might be reminding us of him. Maybe the old Bruiser was one of the people involved."

"Dan! Is it possible?"

"No. We checked. He's in a hospital somewhere in Utah—in traction with broken bones of some kind. Been there three weeks. Fell off a horse while he was making a movie."

"I can't remember how long ago it was I heard Julian talk about 'a bruiser.' It meant something rough, tough, ugly way back when."

"It must have just popped into his head; a way to tell us he wasn't involved in a tea party."

"What else?" she asked, with a tired little shrug of her shoulders.

They sat in silence for a moment.

"Women, down through the ages, have always lost their man," Lydia said, her voice not too steady. "In wars, in accidents, heart attacks, God knows what. Overnight their worlds change. 'Be brave,' their friends tell them."

"So, be brave, doll," Garvey said. "It hasn't happened yet. Early this morning he told you he loved you."

"On tape!"

"That's anyway better than a poke in the eye," Garvey said.

"The thing is, Dan, I wouldn't want to go on without him. It isn't whether I could; I wouldn't want to."

"If you were riding down a mountain in a car and the brakes gave out, who would you like to have driving?" Garvey said.

"Julian," she said promptly.

"A resourceful bastard," Garvey said. "If there's any way out of the jam he's in, Julian's the man to find it. He'll wait, and wait, and choose the very best moment."

"To do what?"

"I wish I could tell you, doll," Garvey said.

CHAPTER SEVEN

Quist and Tatiana talked. There was nothing to do but talk. She had wild ideas about what was to be done. It all involved heroics out of a movie. When Walter brought them lunch trays they would overpower the guard who came with him, take his gun, clobber him and Walter, and run for it.

"I want to get further than the hall outside," Quist said.

He explained to her that there was no way to make a sensible plan until they knew what the second step in it was. There were at least six men, plus the pilot of the chopper and Elliot. There was Walter. There were undoubtedly other servants, as she had suggested. You could run out of one corner and straight into another.

"There are no other houses visible from these windows," Quist said, "nor from the windows of the bedroom where I slept."

"Nothing from my room, either," Tatiana said.

All they knew about the house was this room, the reception hall beyond it, the winding stairway, the hall above, the rooms in which they'd first been held. There was much more to the house than that, but what? Where did these rooms lead to? Certainly there must be a living room, a dining room, a kitchen.

"We need a map," Quist said. "If we could get out into the front hall, out the front door, is there a car we could grab before the whole army surrounds us?"

"So we do nothing. And in the end—?" Tatiana asked.

"In the end we go crazy, try anything," Quist said. "But not just yet." He hesitated to tell her about the tape. It was a long shot, but he hoped Garvey would remember Bruiser Elliot; that they might realize he was passing along the name Elliot to them.

Elliot was not an uncommon name. There were probably hundreds of Elliots in the area. But an Elliot with a helicopter? There was just a chance Garvey, or Kreevich, or the FBI people, if they read "Elliot" in the taped message, might put it together with the helicopter they were obviously searching for. Long, long shot, but a shot.

The talk of escape petered out. Tatiana went on about herself and her father. She had been a child when the Israeli war with Egypt in sixty-seven had driven them out of their home base in the Middle East. Her father had set them up in Paris, from where he handled his elaborate business affairs. It was a world of intrigue, fascinating to the child. Famous men from other countries came and went, dined with them. These famous men needed protection. Men with guns, in the hallways, on the front doorstep, were commonplace. When they rode anyplace in their car, there was always an armed guard up front with the chauffeur.

"I must have heard the death sentence passed on hundreds of people in those days without realizing what I was hearing," Tatiana said. "I would read in the newspapers later that someone who had had lunch at our house last week had been killed in a bombing, at an airport, perhaps, or in a railroad station. Terrorists, they always said. But I begun to guess that the orders had come from our house for that bombing, or for some violence in which many were killed or maimed. Many people could be killed or maimed to hide the real objective, which would be one man."

"Didn't that shock you?"

She gave him a strange bright little smile. "At the time I thought it was pretty remarkable, that my father had so much power. I admired him for it. I still think it's remarkable, but my admiration has dwindled. Especially now. Now I know how easy it will be for him to sign my death warrant—and yours."

"What would touch him? What would reach him?" Quist asked. He was thinking that there might be another tape, another chance, better prepared, to get some kind of clue through to Kreevich and the others.

Tatiana stared out of the closed windows at the lawns and gardens beyond. Talking about her father seemed to give her a kind of perverse pleasure.

"He's touched at this very moment, Julian," she said. "Touched by the fear that he may lose everything that matters to him. He's adding up two columns of figures, two sets of values. On one side is TAIF Oil; on the other side is me. It touches him painfully to have to make any kind of choice. He lives in the sublime belief that he is entitled to everything. He never thinks in terms of 'either-or.' I wish I thought my column of assets was a little longer."

"Love. He's your father," Quist said.

"It just may be that he hates me more than he loves me," the girl said. "If my father ever felt love for another human being it was for my mother, who died giving birth to me. I was to blame for the only real sorrow he ever felt. He ignored me at first, left the care of me to servants and tutors. When I was ten and we had fled to Paris, he finally took an interest in me. He treated me for a little while like a son. That's when the karate lessons began, physical training of all kinds. But I couldn't make it as a boy. When I was twelve he began to try to give me away."

"I don't understand."

Her lovely face was set in hard lines. "A guest in the house in Paris, an important man in my father's world. 'He is a great good friend,' my father told me. 'I would like to show him a special courtesy, offer him special delights. He will come to your room tonight. Do what he asks of you.' And I asked what it was I was expected to do. 'He will teach you,' my father said."

"My God!" Quist said. "Twelve years old?"

She nodded, the corners of her mouth drawn down in a bitter little smile. "So it was, without ever having been taught anything about right or wrong, that I learned about the arts of lovemaking. I wanted to please my father and I guess I was a great success. That success led to another and another night of providing pleasure for my father's special guests."

"What a bastard!" Quist said.

"Oh, I didn't hold it against him then. I guess I thought it was what all women were asked to do. Sometimes there was real pleasure in it, sometimes it was cruel, and clumsy, and even painful. It wasn't until he went away on an extended business trip and I was left in the care of an Englishwoman who was my tutor that I came to understand what had happened to me. My father had turned me into an accomplished prostitute. Oh, I never got any pay for my services, you understand; only my father's grudging approval. But God knows how many big business deals I helped him close."

"It's hard to believe," Quist said.

"You think I'd invent such a story about myself?"

"Arab men are supposed to be paranoid about the untouchableness of their women. To hand you around, like a high class pimp, just doesn't ring true. It would be against his religion, his traditions."

"My father makes his own religion, his own traditions."

"But he would lose face with his people," Quist said.

"God cannot lose face with God," Tatiana said.

"If you're right about him, the chance of his meeting Elliot's ransom demands look rather dim," Quist said.

"Two years ago, when I was eighteen, I took a stand," she said. She laughed. "Women's lib! I would only indulge those friends of my father's who pleased me! Since almost none of them did, I ceased to be very much use to him. That's why my column of assets doesn't add up to very much. So you see, Julian, I am not an innocent little Arab flower girl. But yesterday I began to see that as a value to you and me."

"Value?" his mouth felt dry.

"This man Jones, or Jarvis, has thought of very little else but me since they first brought me to the cabin at the lake. I can see him thinking about how to make his move. I think in this big house he'll find a way. I won't shrink from it. I won't resist his advances. And when he is off guard, I will injure him so badly, physically, that he'll be of no use to himself or to anyone else for a very long time. That may be our moment, Julian, because then I will have his gun!"

Her story was a shocker, her plan was as far out as any of the other notions she'd had, and yet—?

The door to the library was abruptly opened and two of the guards came in, guns at the ready.

"Both of you, back into your rooms upstairs," one of them ordered. Both men seemed to be under some kind of urgent pressure.

A gun in his back, Quist was herded up the stairs and into the room where he'd spent the night. He was left, door locked. He'd had a brief glimpse of Tatiana being taken to the other end of the hall. He had the strong feeling that something was happening to shake the cool operation of Elliot and company. He went to the window, looked down into the garden, and saw that the guards who'd been there were gone. They'd probably been given a break while Quist and Tatiana were being held in the library. Could this be *the* moment, he wondered. And then a man, wearing coveralls and carrying a basket of garden tools, hurried into view. He gave a quick glance at Quist's window and saw him standing there. From the basket of tools he produced a gun and held it up for Quist to see. Then he knelt down and began to work at a garden bed with a hand cultivator.

What Quist couldn't know was that, minutes before, a state trooper's car had come down the drive from the main highway toward the house.

CHAPTER EIGHT

The whole truth about the world in which we live is rarely understood, even by men in high places. Every now and then, like a whale surfacing to spout, we get a glimpse of what may lie beneath the ocean. Political scandals are the most common revelations to the general public. They range from the congressman's secretary, who can't type, to Watergate. An investigative reporter in the Southwest is murdered, and after months and months two men are arrested and convicted. There are whispers—too soft to be heard unless you are the Bionic Woman, with an electronic eardrum, about a senator and his family whom the reporter was investigating—but they die. The senator goes on making highly moral comments in the Senate chamber.

In the sixties college students were shot down on their campuses and in the streets of Chicago, at a national political convention, by federal troops and police. But pious members of the out-party in Washington have let it be known those kids were "radicals," and everyone knows that radicals are "Reds," in league with the Russians to destroy us. The total immorality of a war that wiped out tens of thousands of our young men is brushed under the rug. The complex, devious operations of the world of the Pentagon are no more than that whale spout. The CIA, a vast intelligence operation, run like a spy story written by an adolescent, is wondered about from time to time, particularly when a next-door neighbor finds his phone bugged. There are rumors that J. Edgar Hoover, former head of the FBI, and the man next to God in the American mind, may have used his powerful position for personal gain, may even have framed people of whose politics he disapproved, but he is dead now, so it doesn't really matter, probably isn't true.

Then there is the age of terror in which we are living. Two Kennedys are assassinated, along with Martin Luther King. Governor Wallace of Alabama is shot and crippled for life. In each case a single crackpot is arrested, and sagacious committees announce themselves satisfied that there was no more to it than that—four crackpots. Hostages are taken, bombs are exploded, innocent men, women, and children are tortured and murdered, and the verdict is that the villains are Reds, or Jews, or Arabs, depending on your prejudice.

But there are men who think they know more about the whale than that spout of water he shoots up into a misty sky. One such man was Mark Kreevich of Manhattan's Homicide Squad. He had observed over the years, he had put one fact on top of another, and he had come to the conclusion that major crimes were always related to money and power, private or corporate. It was his job to catch murderers, and he was good at it. He was highly efficient in all the techniques used for catching the man who pulled the trigger, tossed the bomb, set the fire, abducted and killed the child. But he had come to the conclusion that a high percentage of the people he sent to jail were not the real criminals. It was Fagin who taught Charles Dickens's little boys to become pickpockets. Were the "crackpots" who assassinated men in high places the real criminals, or were they only the waterspout from the submerged whale—the real criminal who was never reached or touched? Is the paid assassin the real criminal, or is it the man who pays him and stays comfortably out of sight?

Kreevich was convinced, after many consultations with other police experts, at Interpol, in London, in Paris, and in Rome, that in our society, there was a whole new segment of highly paid, proficient, professional purveyors of violence. Men who took on a violent assignment as casually as a taxi driver picks up a fare. You want a specialist in something, you look in the Yellow Pages. These experts in terror are not to be found there, and yet there must be someplace to find them. Young Ronald James, Feydhev's secretary, had said something about being able to find them "from Tokyo to Warsaw." But if you want to murder a rival political leader, a rival corporate executive; if you want to have Rhaman Feydhev's daughter kidnapped, you don't just go stand on the street corner and wait for someone to come along and offer. Somewhere there were some secret "Yellow Pages": a secret directory where you could find efficient workmen for the job.

Looking for that secret directory had been a hobby of Kreevich's for some time. He suspected that these professional experts in violence must have their own way of advertising. There must be a network of informers in high places who studied the climate of possible crime. Take a political leader who is obviously in big trouble with his opposition. "If I were in your position," a voice whispers in his ear, "I would eradicate the opposition, wipe it out." A joke, maybe? "But who do I get to do it and not have it bounce back on me?" the leader asks. "Well, I know a man who might be helpful." And there is a man ready to be helpful. When the leader gets rid of his conscience, he goes to him.

Kreevich's problem was that no one advertises his skills at murder to an obviously honest police officer. But he had stumbled on something a little while back, a man who would talk a little. Most good police work involves reliable informers. Most informers talk for money or for favors. It's a kind of plea bargaining. The informant stays out of jail as long as he provides usable information.

Samuel Walton was a man out of a storybook. He was enormously fat. Now in his seventies, he was suffering severely from emphysema. To move about at all was to strangle for breath. So he sat, day after day, in his little apartment in Greenwich Village, and watched the world go by—on his television set. But the colors weren't real, he thought, and the world he saw on the screen, in fact or fiction, was not the world he'd known.

Sam Walton had been a courier and actually an espionage agent for the State Department long ago. He had seen the whale. He knew where the bodies were buried and where the closets were that hid the skeletons. He was invaluable to his employers because it was assumed he wouldn't talk to God on Judgment Day about what he knew. But there came a day when he wrestled with his conscience and he threatened to talk. Even Kreevich didn't know what Sam Walton considered telling. The fat man had threatened to talk in order to stop something from happening that he felt endangered national security in some way.

Kreevich had come onto the scene by the purest accident. He had gone to a Pipe Night at The Players, a theatrical club on Gramercy Park. It had been a gay evening, and the homicide man had indulged in a little more alcohol than was his custom. He had decided to walk home from The Players to his apartment in the East Thirties. He'd sleep better, he told himself, for the exercise.

On the way uptown it happened. At a crossing he glanced up a side street and saw a violence. An enormous fat man was down on the sidewalk, and three men were beating and kicking him. In the glare from a streetlight Kreevich caught the glint of a gun, held by the barrel, used as a club; a murder weapon in the right hands.

Kreevich, wearing dinner clothes for the occasion at The Players, was carrying his gun in his overcoat pocket instead of in the usual holster. He had trouble getting it out as he ran toward the violence. He shouted a warning, and that he was a policeman. The man with the gun turned away from beating the fat man with it, tried awkwardly to turn it around in his hand, and was too late. Kreevich brought him down with a bullet in the gut. The other two men ran.

It was an attempted homicide. Sam Walton, badly hurt, went to the emergency ward in St. Vincent's Hospital. In a day or two, when Walton had been moved to a private room, Kreevich went to see him. There were questions that needed asking. He found Sam Walton to be a very engaging man, a man with wit and perpetual good humor. He was also a man who wouldn't talk enough. He worked for the State Department as a courier, he said. Nothing else, although Kreevich was certain there was something else. He suggested that the men who had attacked him were foreign agents. The man whom Kreevich had shot, who was also in the hospital, was as American as apple pie. Kreevich was never able to pry anything out of either man. The attacker repeated over and over that he and his friends, who had escaped, had simply been mugging what looked like a substantial citizen.

It didn't wash, but Kreevich could prove nothing. However, when Sam Walton was able to go home, Kreevich visited him. He had come to like him. He began to get a vague picture of something, but not enough. Someone, high up, had wanted to silence Sam. Who? Sam just smiled a dreamy smile. Kreevich put forward his theory about professionals who were hired by submerged whales all over the world.

"Just know that nothing will persuade me to talk about me," Sam Walton said that night. "But I owe you, Mark. If there is ever anything else—" He smiled. " 'Ask and ye shall receive.' "

So it was that on the third night after the murder of David Peters and the kidnapping of Tatiana Feydhev, and the second night after the disappearance of Julian Quist, Kreevich went to Greenwich Village to visit with his friend Sam Walton.

"I have come to ask, Sam," he said.

Walton was huddled in his big armchair, wheezing for breath. He grinned at his friend. "What kept you?" he said. He gestured toward the television set. "I expected you sooner. You know, Mark, those cigarettes of yours will eventually kill you, and they may kill me. Oh, no, don't stop smoking. I like the smell of the damn things."

Kreevich put out his cigarette but a moment later, not thinking, he lit another.

"The people who did this are not the kidnappers, the murderers," he said. "They are just the people who did the job for somebody else. But Sam, they are not Japanese gunmen, or Poles, or Arabs. They are people who know this city like a book. They also knew the countryside over a hundred miles away, when a cottage would be empty, when the owner would be absent. They knew where to get a helicopter, when my friend Quist blew their cover, and they had a second place to take their prisoners. They are locals. If you were going to hire someone to do a job like this where would you go?"

Sam coughed and struggled for a moment to get his breath. "Have demands been made on Feydhev?"

"Yes."

"What are they?"

"I tell you because I trust you," Kreevich said. "One, twenty million dollars in cash. Two, Feydhev is to put his controlling shares in TAIF Oil on the market, where they will be sold to the highest bidders."

"Wow!" Walton said. "Does he love his daughter that much?"

"He's going through the motions," Kreevich said. "It will take two or three days, he says. The other people seem to know that. It gives us a little time, very little, because I have a feeling he won't come through in the end. Just that much time to save his daughter and my friend. I need to know, Sam, who would have hired out for such a job, who meets my local qualifications."

"Just like that?"

"Just like that."

Sam stared at the darkened screen of his television set. "Only the very best would be hired for a job like this."

"Then God help any of us who hire the second best," Kreevich said. "One of them was idiot enough to shoot an injured dog with the same gun he used on David Peters."

"Not a fast thinker," Sam said. "But if you can't find him?"

"I must find him, Sam, and before he uses it again."

"There are some things I can never tell you, Mark," Sam said. "My sources. So go away somewhere and let me use my phone."

"You think you can come up with the answer?"

"I think I might come up with a half dozen possibilities," Sam said. "The woods are full of these kill-for-hire boys. If I can give you a handful of leads you might get lucky in time. It's the best I can promise you, friend."

CHAPTER NINE

Sergeant Lew Norris of the Vermont State Police was on what he thought of as a routine assignment, not likely to bear fruit. There was a five-state alarm out for a helicopter that might have been used by kidnappers in a big caper, which was all over television, radio, and the newspapers. Police in the surrounding states were also looking. It was the theory of the high command that, if they could eliminate the known choppers in an area, they might narrow the search. The police, particularly in the area near New York, were swamped with well-meaning reports from good citizens about choppers they'd seen between six-thirty and eight-thirty on the critical night, when total darkness took over.

Sergeant Norris's job was fairly simple. In his county there were only seven licensed choppers. Five of them were owned by ski resorts in the mountains. Those five were very active in the winter months, used to spot lost or strayed skiers in the mountains, to locate potential snowslides and set them off before they buried some holiday frolickers, sometimes to carry someone injured in a fall to a hospital in Bennington or Rutland. In summer they were used mostly for pleasure by their owners, but there was no big traffic.

There were two other choppers owned by wealthy residents. One belonged to a lawyer named Cummings, whose summer home was in the mountains, and who flew back and forth to Albany every weekday. His law practice was in the New York State capital. The second belonged to one Brooks Elliot, a businessman—stocks and bonds people said—who had bought the old Simmons estate two years back. Elliot used his chopper to fly back and forth to New York where, it was assumed, he had business on the stock exchange.

Norris was mildly curious about Elliot, who was known to have made some generous contributions to local charities, and who was said to be "a hell of a nice guy." People with money intrigued the sergeant. The Simmons estate, he knew, had been on the market for close to $200,000, and there were the chopper, three or four cars, and servants. Elliot must be rolling in it. Norris was interested because that kind of money was never going to be a part of his life. What was it like, he wondered, to have all that?

The driveway to the house was about half a mile long, from the state highway to the red brick house, with its white colonial columns decorating the front entrance. Norris pulled up his well-marked trooper car about fifty yards from the house. To take it all in, he told himself. The house was built like a capital T, two stories high, with an attic space under a sloping slate roof. You could run a hotel here, Norris thought. There was a six-car garage, a hangar for the chopper. The chopper was in residence, Norris saw. Off to the left was a gardener's or caretaker's cottage. Behind it was a barnlike building. Through open doors Norris could see power lawn mowers, a small tractor, and other maintenance equipment. There was everything here to keep the place looking perfectly manicured.

Norris started to walk toward the house, thinking it was odd that he didn't see anyone around. Place like this there would always be someone working at something, he thought.

Norris was still a few yards from the house, his boot heels crunching on the bluestone driveway, when the front door opened and two men came out and stood waiting for him. One of them he recognized as Brooks Elliot. He'd seen him around town, handsome, wearing plain summer slacks, white sports shoes, a seersucker jacket, and a plaid sports shirt, open at the neck, which matched the slacks. The other man was big, powerful looking, wearing a dark vested city suit.

Kind of odd for a weekend in the country, Norris thought, unless he'd just arrived or was just taking off.

"Good morning, Sergeant," Elliot said, his smile wide and pleasant.

"'Morning, sir," Norris said.

"My friend Mr. Jones, Sergeant. I'm afraid I don't know your name."

"Norris, sir."

"Takes a while to get to know everyone you should," Elliot said. "I could hope policemen would be the last people I'd get to know. Crime isn't my hobby. Or have I committed a crime?" All very light and casual.

"No, sir. Just kind of an unusual check, relating to a crime."

"Check?" Elliot's smile was still there, but there was a curious, hard brightness to the look he gave the trooper.

"You probably saw on television or read in the paper about a murder and kidnapping in New York," Norris said. "Daughter of some big oil man snatched, her boyfriend shot."

Jones muttered something under his breath that Norris didn't catch. "What did you say, sir?" he asked.

"I said, 'Oh, brother!' " Jones said.

"Nasty business," Norris said. "They holed up in a cabin about sixty, seventy miles away from here in Massachusetts. A man named Quist stumbled on their hideout and they took him, too. Police down there think they took off in a helicopter."

Elliot's laugh was soft. "My helicopter, Sergeant?"

"Oh, no, sir," Norris said. "But one way to narrow the field is to check on all the helicopters within a hundred miles of that place in Massachusetts. People keep phoning to tell us that they heard or saw a chopper here, another there. If we can find out what choppers were up and where they put down, we can eliminate the false alarms."

"So you want to know where my chopper was yesterday evening, between six-thirty and dark?" Elliot asked.

"That's it, sir. Just routine. There are only seven choppers in the area. We've had calls, however, people saying they heard something around dark. You're the last one on my list. All the others are accounted for."

Jones moved. If Norris had noticed, he would have seen that the man in the business suit had shifted his feet, planting them like a fighter waiting for the first punch in the next round. He might also have noticed that Jones was playing with the lapel on the left side of his jacket.

"As a matter of fact, my copter was up about that time," Elliot said, "bringing me back from New York. I recall we had to have lights shone on us from below in order to land. Could have been eight-thirty, quarter to nine."

"You've got landing lights?" Norris asked.

Elliot laughed. "No. We just circle around and one of my men waves an electric torch around from the center of the landing pad over there. That's all you need to put down a chopper, Sergeant."

"You were flying it, sir?"

"No, I have a pilot who flies a kind of taxi service for me."

"I suppose he keeps a log, a record of his flights. I mean, when he took you to New York, where the chopper was while you did your business, when you took off from there for home."

"I suppose he does. It's a regulation, isn't it?"

"Yes, it is." Norris chuckled, quite relaxed. "It would show you didn't stop at Lake Toromog on your way home."

"Oh, brother!" Jones said again. He was flexing the fingers of his right hand.

"It certainly would, Sergeant," Elliot said easily. "Unfortunately my pilot has taken the day off. I had no need for him. He won't check in until tomorrow, and I have no idea where he keeps his log. I could have it for you tomorrow."

"Oh, I guess that won't be necessary, Mr. Elliot. You tell me you were in New York and flew back just after dark, that's good enough for me. That satisfies one call."

"Call?"

"Someone heard a chopper about that time, phoned us. So it was yours."

"Must have been."

"I wonder," Norris said, almost apologetically, "if I could take a look at her?"

" 'Her,' Sergeant?"

"The chopper. Just my own private curiosity, sir. I've always been fascinated by flying machines. Been taking flying lessons myself. One of these days—" He shrugged.

"Help yourself," Elliot said.

The trooper gave them a casual salute and headed toward the chopper in its hangar. At the same moment, a noisy mowing machine came out of the barn and began to circle around the lawn between Elliot and the trooper car. The figure in coveralls was Breslin, driving the mower.

"The sonofabitch is onto us," Jones said to Elliot. "Flying lessons, my ass!"

"I don't think so," Elliot said, frowning. "Just a country boy."

"Look at him!" Jones said, over the noise of the mower. "He's examining the landing gear!"

"So what?"

"Maybe we picked up something back there at the lake."

"What?"

"How do I know. You can't let him go, Elliot." And Jones pulled his gun out of the holster under his left armpit.

"Cut it out, Jarvis!" Elliot ordered, moving between Jones and the trooper in the hangar.

Norris straightened up, waved to them, and headed toward his car.

"He'll bring the whole damn county down on us!" Jones said. He raised his gun to bring it down in a classic aim position.

Elliot grabbed at his arm, literally wrestling with him. "You crazy bastard," he said.

The noisy lawn mower swerved in close to them. Breslin was shouting something they couldn't hear. In the struggle between Elliot and Jones the gun went off. The mower covered the sound of the shot in part, and it was also deadened because the gun was pressed right against Elliot's stomach when it went off. The mower also covered the sound of Elliot's scream.

Jones grabbed Elliot and held him up. The mower swirled in front of them, throwing up a cloud of grass.

At his car, Sergeant Norris looked back and waved. Odd, he thought. The two guys looked as if they were dancing with each other.

PART THREE

CHAPTER ONE

Inaction was intolerable to Dan Garvey. He sat on the terrace of Quist's apartment with Lydia, talking round and round the same circles. Like dogs chasing their tails, they were getting nowhere. Kreevich was not answering his phone when they called, either at home or at his office. As if he might have something new every ten minutes! Quist wasn't suddenly going to call them, full of happy news. Not unless the case was over. It was clear there were long hours to wait while Rhaman Feydhev prepared himself for the moment of decision. The only good thing about that was it justified the hope that Julian was alive and still being treated well, as he'd indicated on the tape.

The twilight had the warm, pinkish look of a summer evening.

Garvey stood up, abruptly. "I wouldn't want to go to Philadelphia for my own funeral," he said. "But I'm going to Philadelphia."

"Dan, why?" Lydia asked. She urgently wanted not to be left alone, but she tried not to show it.

"Cannikin, he bothers me," Garvey said.

"I don't understand."

"Fits too neatly," he said. "His unusual job for a whole week. He usually does just one-night stands, concerts. The people we want didn't just pick his cabin by chance. They've done nothing by chance. They knew he'd be gone, knew he wouldn't come back."

"But he did come back. To look for his dog."

"What would that matter, if he knew they were there. If he made a deal with them to use his camp, he was the one person they didn't have to worry about if he showed up. If he made a deal with them, he knows who they are."

"Dan, I watched him. I don't believe it. The only thing he was interested in was his dog."

"He's a professional actor," Garvey said. "Look, doll, there's nothing to do but turn over stones to look for maggots! No point in leaving one unturned, is there? I've got something going for me in Philadelphia. Cannikin is appearing at the Park Garden. It's a music tent just outside the city. We put Julie Haynes in there last summer, remember?"

Lydia nodded. Julie Haynes was a singer client.

"So I know the manager there, Joey Mandel. I'd like to ask him how come he booked Cannikin for a week. Not his usual policy."

"Call him on the phone," Lydia said.

"I want to really talk," Garvey said. "If something sounds fishy Cannikin will be there to answer questions. Ed Parks can fly me down. Seven-thirty now, I'll be there by nine, nine-thirty. Talk a while, follow up on that talk, back here by one."

"It sounds like a long shot," Lydia said.

"I never thought I'd duck a chance to spend time with you," Garvey said. "But I just can't stand doing nothing about Julian. I'd ask you to go with me, but I know you won't."

"I can't, Dan. If Julian found a way to get in touch and I wasn't here—!"

Ed Parks was a pilot employed by the sports arena on the Island, Garvey's special project for Julian Quist Associates. The Arena owned a small plane. No problem if Ed could be reached. He could; he would arrange a clearance and call Philadelphia while Garvey was getting out to the Island. The flight to Philadelphia would take less time than it would take Garvey to get out to the Island.

At ten minutes to nine Garvey walked up to the box office of the Park Garden and asked for Joey Mandel. Inside he could hear Cannikin's high, clear voice, the guitar accompaniment, the young-girl hysteria.

Mandel was standing at the back of the tent, "counting the house." Looking at Joey, you might have taken him for a small-time bookmaker, a just slightly dishonest con artist. He was balding, overdressed, overconfident. He would, Garvey thought, be easy to puncture if he was mixed up in something.

"Dan! What are you doing here?" Joey's handshake was professionally cordial.

"Came to ask you something about the 'Great Man,'" Garvey said, gesturing toward the stage at Cannikin, who was performing in a white suit with glittering spangles.

"I got to admit he brings them in," Mandel said.

"What do you mean you've got to admit?" Garvey asked. "You hired him."

"Well, sure. But you never know."

"So you didn't know, so you booked him in for a full week?"

"What's eating you, Dan? You sound mad at me," Mandel said.

Garvey realized he was letting his tensions get the better of him. "You ever look at TV or read a newspaper, Joey? If you do, you know that a gang of murdering kidnappers, who also hijacked my boss, used Cannikin's cabin up in Massachusetts as a hideout."

"Hey, that's right. You know, Dan, I didn't think about Quist for a minute. Only the girl and the guy they killed."

"I think about Quist," Garvey said.

"Any news?" Joey asked.

"We think Quist and the girl were alive this morning."

A great moaning and squealing went up in the audience, as if a couple of thousand young women had been simultaneously titillated in their most sensitive sexual zones. Cannikin had gone into his own version of the Frank Sinatra hit, "I Did It My Way."

Joey Mandel was applauding. He should not be seen not applauding, but his attention was fixed on Garvey. "You think buster up there could be involved? No, Dan. He makes so much money the honest way—if you can call what he's doing up there honest. He stole the whole phrasing of that song from Old Blue Eyes."

"But he's younger and got better hips to swivel than Sinatra," Garvey said. "How much are you paying him, Joey?"

Joey looked proud. "Six performances, thirty-six Gs." He laughed. "You don't have to add kidnapping to that kind of bread to be rich and happy."

"Percentage of the take?"

"Flat fee."

"You don't take that kind of gamble, Joey. I've dealt with you, remember?"

"Yeah, that Haynes broad. She did well, Danno."

"But on a percentage basis. Come clean, Joey. How come this flat fee deal with Cannikin? It's important for me to know, chum."

Cannikin had finished his number and was blotting at his face with a white silk handkerchief. The audience was standing, clapping and screeching. Joey looked unhappy.

"You think Cannikin might be involved in your thing?" he asked.

"He might be," Garvey said.

Cannikin waved the audience back to its seats and began one of his own smash hits, "Little Lost Boy."

"Well, there was something kind of screwy about it," Joey said. "I mean, you're right. I couldn't risk that kind of deal for Cannikin or anyone else. Percentage up to that amount, maybe, but not a flat fee. But this guy called me on the phone."

"What guy?"

"Would you believe I don't know? He never gave me a name. He said he had reasons for wanting Cannikin to put in a week here. I should give him whatever he asked and he, the caller, would make up whatever I lost on the deal. I told him it could be twelve, fifteen thousand bucks. He told me he'd deliver me fifteen grand and I could keep the change. I should make a deal with Cannikin and let him know when it was closed."

"How were you to let him know?"

" 'Don't call us, we'll call you,' " Joey said, quoting an old theatrical cliché. "A couple of hours later, a messenger delivered a package for me. In it was fifteen grand in nice new bills."

"No name?"

"No name. I forgot to tell you, Cannikin was not to know anyone else was in on the deal. 'It would hurt his pride,' the guy said on the phone."

"Thoughtful of him."

"Guys like Cannikin have strange admirers, both sexes," Mandel said. "So Cannikin bit and I booked him for this week. The next morning this guy called me on the phone again and I told him it was all settled."

"Still no name?"

"Mandel laughed. "It could have been Santa Claus the way things look. Cannikin keeps pulling them in the way he has, the whole of that fifteen Gs should go into my greedy little pocket."

"Does Cannikin have an agent?"

"Sure. Bill Hancock. Cannikin put me onto him when I tried to book him. Hancock drew up the contract and must have been laughing all the way to the bank."

Garvey knew Hancock, a legitimate operator with a very good reputation in the field. No trick stuff from him. "Santa Claus" was the guy Garvey was after, but how to find him?

Cannikin's performance at the Park Garden ended a little before eleven. It took a bodyguard of ushers to get him through the crowd of salivating girls to his dressing room. Garvey found him there, wringing wet, looking like an athlete who had just won the Boston marathon. This kid, whatever you thought of his material, gave it all he had. He earned his money, Garvey thought.

A bath towel wrapped around his neck, Cannikin looked up at the visitor in his dressing room. It wasn't unreasonable that he didn't seem to recognize Garvey for a moment. Garvey hadn't been in the foreground at Lake Toromog. Cannikin was trying to make some other association with a vaguely familiar face. Then he got it.

"Julian Quist's friend," he said.

"Dan Garvey," Garvey said.

"Look, Mr. Garvey, give me a couple of minutes in the shower. You mind? I could catch my death sitting around in these wet clothes."

Cannikin went into a shower room adjoining the dressing room. Garvey waited, wondering if he'd given the singer time to think up the wrong answers to the right questions. Cannikin reappeared, wearing a bright orange bathrobe, still toweling his blond hair, which seemed to curl naturally as he dried it.

"Is there something new?" he asked. "I imagine you're not down here to listen to me sing."

"But what I heard was good," Garvey said. "I never had a couple of thousand dames trying to unzip my fly."

"Name of the game," Cannikin said. He sat down at his dressing table, giving Garvey a hard, level stare.

"The people who took over your cabin had it carefully planned," Garvey said. "They knew you were going to be here for a week. If it hadn't been for your dog and Quist they'd probably still be there. They had to make the whole thing match with the moment they chose for the kidnapping. They didn't just stumble on an empty cabin. It had to be planned."

"So?" Cannekin said.

"My first thought was that you had loaned your camp to friends," Garvey said. He held up his hand as Cannikin started to interrupt. "Maybe quite innocently, unaware of why they wanted to use it."

"No!" Cannikin said sharply.

"I've just heard something from Joey Mandel that helps me to believe you." Garvey outlined the story of the "Santa Claus" call. "Tell me your side of how the deal was made."

Cannikin put aside his towel. "Mandel called me. That is, he got a message to me at the camp, where there is no phone, and I called him collect. He offered me a booking for a week. I didn't want to do a week, so I set a high price on it. He accepted. I told him my agent would draw up the contract."

"Bill Hancock?"

"Yes. Bill told me I'd accepted too quickly. If Mandel wanted me that badly he'd have paid more. But I'd agreed. That's all of it. I don't get it, Mr. Garvey. Someone paid Mandel a bonus to get me working here for a week?"

"Those are the lyrics," Garvey said.

"I don't get it."

"It's simple enough," Garvey said. "For some reason, the kidnappers chose the Lake Toromog area to hole up. They had to find a camp that wasn't occupied. With you they could make sure. They could arrange for a job that would keep you away. These people aren't hurting for money, you understand. They're aiming at taking over an empire."

"Why Lake Toromog? There are dozens of camps, lots of people coming and going. You'd think they'd have looked for an isolated place."

"Perhaps because some of them would be coming and going while they tried to make their deal for the girl," Garvey said. "Comings and goings might be noticed in an isolated place."

"But Quist stumbled on them, and I would have later if he hadn't," Cannekin said.

"Even a criminal genius can't forsee the little things," Garvey said. "The house that Jack built. If it hadn't been for a marauding fox hunting wild ducks, a man named Fahnestock wouldn't have set a trap; if he hadn't set a trap, your dog would have been home when you left for Philadelphia and safely with the lady who boards him when you are away. If your dog, caught in the trap, hadn't tried to struggle home for help, Quist wouldn't have heard his cries of pain. I'm sure that's what happened. Quist heard him, followed him, found himself outside your cabin. Someone shot the dog and took Quist prisoner. So the whole thing goes back to a fox the criminals couldn't foresee."

"Goddamn them," Cannikin said. "Charlie Brown meant more to me than anything."

"And Quist means more to me," Garvey said.

CHAPTER TWO

Outside Brooks Elliot's house in the Vermont hills a white-faced Jarvis-Jones was trying to hold up Elliot, who was sagging, deadweight, in his arms. Breslin, watching the retreating Sergeant Norris, kept the power mower circling, screaming over the noise of its motor at Jones.

At last Sergeant Norris's car disappeared along the main highway, apparently unhurried. Breslin shut off the power mower and ran to the other two men.

"You crazy damned idiot!" He shouted at Jones.

Together they lowered Elliot to the grass. An angry red stain grew in the area of the wounded man's stomach.

"We got to get out of here," Jones said. "That cop has us smelled out."

"So you shot the only guy who can figure an out for us!" Breslin said. He knelt beside Elliot, a hand under the man's head. "Boss, can you hear me? It's Breslin!"

Elliot's eyes were closed. He wasn't hearing anything.

"He tried to stop me," Jones muttered. "Pulled the goddamn gun right down into his own gut. I didn't mean to shoot him, but my finger was hooked onto the trigger and he was—was pulling at me."

"Let's get him into the house, see what we can do for him." Breslin's face was chalk white.

Between them, Breslin and Jones lifted the unconscious man and carried him toward the house. The front door opened before they reached it and Walter, the tongueless black man, was there, making strange inarticulate sounds. Behind him were two of the bodyguards. Walter bent over the wounded man, making crooning noises. Then he straightened up and gestured frantically toward the library.

He led the way, almost dancing in his anxiety. He reached the big couch ahead of them, placed a pillow for Elliot's head. He made anxious gestures they couldn't read.

Elliot moaned as they lowered him to the coach.

"He isn't dead," Jones said.

Walter bent down again, unfastened Elliot's belt, and with surprisingly gentle hands he pulled up the man's shirt and undershirt, revealing an ugly wound that was seeping blood.

The two men looked at each other with a kind of helplessness. Walter, mumbling and muttering, ran out of the room. Moments later he was back, carrying a basin of water and some clean white cloths. He knelt beside the couch and, gentle but clumsy, did what he could to clean the wound and stop the bleeding. He looked up at Breslin, his eyes wide, and shook his head, urgently.

"He's hurt bad," Breslin said.

Walter nodded vigorously, making his anxious sounds.

"He needs a doctor," Breslin said. "For Christ sake, I know that, Walter. So we call a local doctor, he reports a gunshot wound to cops, and we've had it. If they dig out the slug and get lucky with it, they'll discover it's at least the third time you've used that gun, Jarvis."

"I tell you, that cop that was here is already calling out the marines," Jarvis-Jones said.

"If he is, we won't get half a mile down the main highway before we hit a roadblock," Breslin said.

"The chopper," Jarvis-Jones said.

"You fly it, Butch?" Breslin asked bitterly. "Dixon won't be back till tomorrow morning. If someone here could fly the damn thing, we could take Elliot down to the city. There are doctors there who won't talk. Check with the other boys, Jarvis. Somebody may have a talent we don't know about."

Walter made excited sounds and gestured wildly toward the ceiling.

"You can fly it, Walter?" Breslin asked.

Violent negative head shakes and more pointings at the ceiling.

"Get on with it, Jarvis," Breslin said. "Let's see if we get lucky for a change."

Jarvis-Jones left the room, muttering to himself. Walter seemed to be beside himself. He gestured to Breslin to take over with the hot water and cloths and then hurried out of the room again. He came back almost at once, carrying a newspaper. He pointed at an article on the front page, mouth working over his inarticulate sounds. He kept jabbing a finger at the article in the paper.

Breslin saw that it was an account of the murder and the kidnapping and the abduction of Quist.

"So what?" Breslin said.

Walter held a black finger on a line in the article. He was almost praying at Breslin to read it. Finally Breslin concentrated on what Walter kept pointing at. After the account of Quist's disappearance there was a paragraph:

> Julian Quist, well-known public relations expert, who graduated from Columbia University in 1958, is a captain in the U.S. Air Force Reserve, and has promoted some of the most famous people in the theater, in films, and in politics. Julian Quist Associates also handles promotion for such well-known corporations as HAPCO, American Utilities, and Roulard, the famous cosmetics empire. The new sports arena on Long Island is also—"

Walter kept jabbing at the center of the paragraph, word after word. Finally it dawned on Breslin. ". . . captain in the U.S. Air Force Reserve . . ."

"Jesus!" Breslin muttered.

Walter nodded, smiling. Sweat ran down off his eager face.

"Get Jarvis and the others in here," Breslin said, and the black man took off on the run.

Breslin sat on the edge of the couch, holding a wet cloth against Elliot's stubbornly bleeding wound. His face looked as if it had been dusted with ashes.

Upstairs in his elegant bedroom, Quist felt time dragging by. He turned on his television set on the hour for the news, but there was simply a "nothing new" on the story that concerned him. Sparkey Lyle had saved another game for the Yankees; Jack Nicklaus was leading in the second round of this week's big golf tournament; the Middle East oil cartel was threatening a rise in oil prices. But "nothing new" on the fate of two lives in the hands of murdering kidnappers.

Quist had been interested for a while in the changing of the guard in the garden below his windows. He sensed that something was up. The hurried retreat from the library, a new guard pretending to be a gardener. The best guess was that somebody unexpected had appeared on the property. A cop never occurred to him. He heard the power mower going but he couldn't see from his window where it was operating. Eventually the gardening guard was replaced by the two men who had been there before. Whatever the crisis had been, it was apparently over. He wondered what had become of Walter. The service was deteriorating. It was long past time for lunch.

At last he heard the lock in his door turn. It was Jones, looking his ugly self, gun at the ready, as always.

"Back downstairs," Jones said.

"Anything for exercise," Quist said.

Every time he saw Jones, Quist knew this big man with the gun was the most dangerous obstacle to any move he might contrive at the last moment. He found himself studying the way the man walked, the way he handled his gun. He knew that when the time came there'd be no second chance.

In the reception hall downstairs, two of the guards were standing outside the library door, huddled in a conversation. They broke it up as Quist approached and went through the door into the library.

Breslin was there, and Walter was kneeling by the couch. The man lying on the couch was Elliot. Quist saw a blood-stained cloth, discarded and lying on the floor beside the couch. Quist moved closer and saw the gaping wound in Elliot's stomach.

"What happened?" he asked.

"An accident," Breslin said.

Quist turned his head. "One of Jones's accidents?"

Jones glared at him, the gun suddenly dangerous.

"The man needs a doctor," Breslin said.

"So get him one. And I advise quickly, from the way it looks," Quist said.

"We can't call a local man," Breslin said. "He'd report a gunshot wound to the state police."

"Dilemma," Quist said.

Breslin picked up a newspaper that was lying on the reading table beside him. "Piece about you here," he said.

"I hope they spelled my name right," Quist said.

"It says here, 'U.S. Air Force Reserve.' That means you're a flyer, doesn't it?"

Quist stared at the man, not believing what he'd heard and what it implied.

"Yes, I can fly a plane," he said very quietly.

"Choppers?"

"Yes."

"We want you to fly Elliot to New York where we can get medical help that won't kick back at us," Breslin said.

Quist couldn't believe his ears. "You have to be kidding," he said. "Why don't you just drive him out?"

"The state police have been here. We're not sure about them. There may be roadblocks."

"And I'm to fly Elliot and some of you out?"

"That's it," Breslin said.

"What about the girl?" Quist asked.

"We hang onto her to keep you honest," Jones said, from behind him.

Quist turned. He was smiling. "Since you have no intention of letting me out of this alive, what's to prevent my dumping all of us in the Hudson River, or up against a hillside? I might as well die happy, you know."

"Bastard!" Jones said.

"Another dilemma," Quist said.

One of the other guards, a slim, ash blond with very pale blue eyes, spoke his piece. "Is there no way we can reach Dixon?" he asked.

"Shacked up with some dame in the city, God knows where," Breslin said. "He's been on call, round the clock, for the last ten days. Elliot thought it was safe to give him twenty-four hours off. We didn't expect to have to leave here for a couple of days."

"So we wait for him," the blond said. "I wouldn't ride around the block with this character." He indicated Quist.

"If that trooper who was here is wise to us, Whitey, we haven't got any time to wait for anyone or anything," Breslin said. "I personally don't think the man came up with anything. He was checking choppers in the area, routine. Cops are checking on choppers in five states, I understand. There's nothing about ours to arouse suspicion."

"He was looking at the landing gear," Jones said. "How do you know what it shows? He wouldn't have tried to take us alone. He's gone for help."

"While you argue about it," Quist said to no one in particular, "your friend Elliot is bleeding to death."

Walter, the black man, made vehement sounds that were meant to agree.

"Not that I have any reason to wish him well," Quist said. "But he needs help and in a hurry. I've got a hunch that moving him around, flying or driving him to New York without a doctor first, is the ball game for him. What's the matter, Breslin, you lost without Elliot to tell you what to do?"

"You know anything about first aid?" Breslin asked.

"Band-Aids and iodine are about my limit," Quist said. "Don't they train you boys how to put out the fire after they've given you the matches?"

A heavy hand grabbed Quist's shoulder and spun him around. Jones's anger was at the exploding point. "So go ahead, make jokes!" he said.

CHAPTER THREE

FBI Agent Frank Rubek sat facing Rhaman Feydhev in the suite at the Beaumont in New York. Lieutenant Mark Kreevich stood by the windows, looking at the antlike figures on the sidewalk twenty-five floors down. He had called his friend Sam Walton several times since the night before.

"I'm sorry, Mark," the fat man kept telling him. "My source is out of town, expected back sometime today. We just have to wait till I can talk to him."

"Time's running out, Sam."

"I know," the fat man said. Kreevich could hear the endless struggle for breath going on in the Greenwich Village apartment. "It's all I can do, Mark—wait for my source."

Kreevich had sources of his own, others beside Sam Walton. It was said of him that he knew the criminal patterns of his city better than any other man in police work. But the well was dry when it came to this case. Kreevich thought he understood why. The plan to strip Feydhev of his wealth and power had been made across the world from here. Somewhere, oceans away, men waited for the word that Feydhev had come across with the money demanded, and that the invaluable shares in TAIF Oil were about to come on the market. These men, shaded somewhere from the hot Middle East sun and police scrutiny, had hired mercenaries to handle the overt criminal aspects of the plan, foot soldiers who were only minor figures in a conspiracy. These foot soldiers, Kreevich thought, must be in constant contact with the master schemers across the world. How? By overseas telephone? Calls relayed from London to Paris to Rome to where? The steps he and Rubek were taking here were too vague, too complicated, too cumbersome. Sam Walton might come up with half a dozen suggestions from his source of men in this country who could be hired for a kidnapping. By the time each of them was traced down it would be long past the deadline for Feydhev. Could Feydhev stall beyond tomorrow or the next day? The state police of five states were trying to track down a helicopter, one out of hundreds that had been in the air at the critical time. There wasn't the manpower to accomplish this in time without the wildest kind of good luck. Nothing that they were doing stood any real chance of succeeding in time.

A slow-burning anger was eating away at Kreevich. A lead to the main conspirators, across the oceans somewhere, could come from only one source, Feydhev. Feydhev must have a clear notion of who was out to steal his world. Rubeck had tried to get that information from Feydhev without success. As far as Kreevich could tell, Feydhev had made certain key moves. The cash had been withdrawn from various banks. Twenty million dollars in cash in several black bags was stored in one of the inner rooms of the suite. How TAIF Oil finally came on the market was a financial operation that Kreevich hadn't bothered with. There would be brokers, probably completely honest guys, in stock markets here and abroad, ready to bid on the TAIF stock when it was offered for sale. *If* it was offered for sale! Kreevich was convinced Feydhev had no intention of going that far when the deadline was reached.

Kreevich turned from the windows to look at the Arab oil millionaire. He sat, stiff backed and grim faced, drumming with impatient fingers on the arms of his chair. Agent Rubek was going over and over the ground, trying to pry something out of Feydhev that might be useful. Feydhev had the same answer, repeated like an automation. "I can't answer that question, Mr. Rubek." Or "That is a confidential matter, Mr. Rubek."

Kreevich had had it. He walked across the room and stood in front of the big armchair, looking down at Feydhev. The oil tycoon looked at the detective with a kind of weary contempt. You could see in his face, in his burning black eyes, that he felt he was being annoyed by incompetent amateurs. He was playing his own game and he would play it his own way.

"It seems pretty clear to me, Mr. Feydhev, that you have no real concern for your own daughter," Kreevich said. "Neither do I, except that she is a piece with a name on a chessboard. A piece in a game I don't intend to lose. But there is someone, a friend, held with your daughter, about whom I do care. He's flesh and blood to me, and what you do may be a matter of life and death to him. I'm sick of playing games with you, Feydhev. We need help, we need facts."

Feydhev sighed, a sound that reflected his weariness at dealing with something that seemed immaterial to him.

"I appreciate your concern for your friend, Lieutenant," he said, in a cold, emotionless voice, "even though you accuse me of having no concern for Tatiana. What you think of me, or what you think my feelings are doesn't matter to me."

"There is one good chance of winning this game for all of us," Kreevich said. "The more I listen to Rubek the more I'm convinced of it. The professional terrorists who are holding your daughter and my friend must be in contact with the man, or men, who have hired them for the job. The only way to be in contact in a short stretch of time, three days we think, is by phone. But it is hopeless to try to monitor the thousands of calls that go overseas every day on the chance that we will pick up a few words from someone to someone that might have meaning for us. But if we knew who might be receiving those calls at the other end, we'd have a chance to locate the people at this end. Let me put it to you, Feydhev, that your refusal to help us in every way you can makes you an accomplice in one murder we know about and two more that seem likely."

Feydhev's heavy eyelids closed for a moment, as if he were praying for patience. Then his lids lifted and he looked straight at Kreevich with his smouldering eyes. "I'm going to say this to you once, and only once, Lieutenant. I care for my daughter more than you know. She is not a piece on a chessboard to me. She is mine, my child. But I am a realist, Lieutenant. While you and Mr. Rubek dream of heroic rescue and brilliant police work, I face facts. The people who are holding my daughter and your friend are professionals. You've said that yourself, again and again. Is that anything but a word to you, Lieutenant? I'll tell you what it means to me. It means men who have no concern for human life, except their own. They expect to be paid handsomely for what they've done, and they don't intend to be caught—not by you, not by the FBI, not by anyone. At the end of three days of capture, of being moved from one place to another, Tatiana and your friend will know enough about them to hang them." Feydhev took a deep breath. "So you see, it will not matter to Tatiana or to your friend whether I meet their demands or not. They have already been sentenced to death." Suddenly both hands came down hard on the arms of his chair. "I assume my daughter is dead, Lieutenant—or will be dead, no matter what I do. My plans, my thinking, are based on that assumption."

"Until it is a fact, I say there is a chance," Kreevich said.

"That is the naïve thinking of a child, Lieutenant."

"Give us the names of your enemies," Kreevich said. "You must have been dreaming of them ever since your daughter was taken. They must be on the tip of your tongue."

"My daughter and your friend are dead, or as good as dead," Feydhev said. "You want the truth from me, Lieutenant? I have no intention of paying the money or making any stock available for sale. I have gone through the motions to gain time. You asked for time, I wanted it." A deep, almost fierce anger took control of his voice. "Do you imagine for a moment that I intend to let this butchery go unpunished? I have my own people, Lieutenant. The people responsible for this are going to pay, one by one, until I've wiped them off the face of the earth."

It was a kind of terrible power talking, something Kreevich understood as a fact of life but not as a human emotion.

"Give us a chance," he said. "Give us names! Overnight we might come up with something that would help us before it's too late."

"It is already too late," Feydhev said. "If they are still alive and you can find a house where they're being held, they will see you coming and Tatiana and your friend will be shot dead before you can knock on the door."

"Give us a chance to try," Rubek said.

"I tell you, there is no chance," Feydhev said. "Suppose I give you names, and suppose tomorrow, or in a week, or in a month, the men to whom those names are attached begin to disappear from the face of the earth? What would happen to your conscience then, Lieutenant? Yours, Mr. Rubek? Honest children! You would let it be known that I had given you the names, that I must be responsible. No, Lieutenant, this is a war, a revenge, that I have to handle in my own way."

"Even before we know for sure what has happened to your daughter and my friend?"

"I know for sure, Lieutenant. Depend on it. I know for sure. I know how these people work; how they always have and always will."

Kreevich turned away. It was a look into the dark corners of the minds of men who lived by violence, accepted it as a way of life.

CHAPTER FOUR

It was not, Quist had to concede, a time for jokes. He stood looking at Jones, whose hand was gripping his shoulder like an iron claw; a man out of control. Someone had chosen badly when this gun-happy goon had been selected as a member of a team involved in what might be a billion-dollar crime. He had added murder to a kidnapping in the very first move outside the Beaumont in New York. He had wiped out a carefully planned hideway at Lake Toromog by shooting a helpless dog and taking a dangerous prisoner. Now he had deprived the others of the man who was obviously the master planner of one phase of the crime. Jones, gun in hand, was a menace to friend and foe alike. Quist sensed that one more jibe at this psychotic murder machine and he would be the next victim.

"I have a suggestion," Quist said.

"It better be good," Jones said. He let go his hold on Quist's shoulder. Quist was aware of a kind of group relaxing of tensions. Breslin, who had taken a step toward them, turned away. Whitey took a handkerchief out of his pocket and wiped at his face with it. Walter, frozen for a moment, turned back to the wounded man, crooning over him like an anxious mother.

"None of you seems to know what to do about your friend on the couch," Quist said. "God knows I don't, except that someone's got to dig that bullet out of him if you want him to live. I remember reading somewhere that it takes a man six to ten minutes to bleed to death—if he's really bleeding."

Walter made moaning sounds. He was holding a bloodied cloth tightly over Elliot's wound.

"There's somebody you haven't tried, who just might know something," Quist said.

"Who?" Breslin asked.

"The girl. Miss Feydhev."

"Oh, for God sake!" Jones said. "That crazy-talking bitch!"

"I might as well tell you I discovered she speaks English as well as you do."

"Why should she know anything about first aid?" Breslin asked.

"She comes from a part of the world where they shoot people for breakfast," Quist said. "Women all over the globe take nursing courses. It's a chance. You could ask her."

"Bring her down here," Breslin said to Whitey.

The blond gunman took off.

Anything for time, Quist thought. Anything to cool off the explosive potential of the moment. Anything to give Breslin a chance to think his way through the jam they were all in. Anything to lessen the chance that some kind of spark would set Jones in motion again.

Breslin was looking down over Walter's shoulder at Elliot. "We've got to find some way to bring him to," he said. "He's our only way to contact the people with the money."

"I know that!" Jones said. "Why did he have to get in my way?"

"Because you wouldn't listen to him," Breslin said. "Goddamn, I almost had the money spent!"

The man named Whitey brought Tatiana into the library, almost dragging her by the arm. She looked, anxiously, for some sort of cue from Quist.

"I've told our friends that you suddenly remembered this morning that you speak English," Quist said. "They've got big troubles. I suggested you might be able to help." He gestured toward the man on the couch.

She could have reacted any number of ways. She could have been frightened by the sight of blood and the sick, sweet smell of it. She could have denied any knowledge of what to do about it. Instead, she seemed to make an effort to pull herself together and then walked over to stand by Walter. The black man looked up at her, hope in that look.

"Is that water boiled?" she asked in a cool, practical voice.

Walter shook his head.

"Get some boiled water and more clean cloths," she said.

Walter hurried off, relieved at having a definite assignment. Tatiana lifted a bloody cloth from the wound. Quite a girl, Quist thought. She didn't flinch at the ugly wound. She turned to Breslin.

"Gunshot wound?" she asked.

"Yes."

"Bullet still in the wound?"

"Yes."

"That's beyond me," Tatiana said. "You need a doctor, and in a hurry."

"Do I have to tell you that we can't call a local doctor?"

"Then you have to arrange to bury him somewhere," Tatiana said, in that same cool voice.

"We plan to drive or fly him out of here to New York," Breslin said.

"He won't make it," Tatiana said. She had reached down and her fingers were on Elliot's pulse. "I can clean the wound. I may be able to do something to stop the bleeding. But I can't dig for that bullet. I wouldn't know how. I could kill him right there on the couch."

No one spoke.

"Do you have any brandy, whiskey?" Tatiana asked. "His pulse is very flighty."

"Whitey!" Breslin said.

Once again the blond guard hurried out of the room. In the doorway he passed Walter, who was returning with a fresh basin of water and clean cloths.

Breslin glanced at his watch. "It must be a good forty-five minutes since that cop left here," he said. "Elliot was right. He didn't tumble to anything. Goddamn you, Jarvis!"

Jones stood watching, stonefaced.

Tatiana knelt by Elliot and began to work on the wound with the clean materials Walter had brought. "It's very deep," she said, and for the first time her voice wasn't quite steady.

Quist's mind was racing around with impossibles. A quick lurch at Jones? One chance in a hundred of getting his gun? A run for it, he and Tatiana? There were at least three other men he had seen, who were somewhere outside. They would get just exactly nowhere.

Whitey came back, carrying a bottle of brandy and a shot glass.

"Lift him, very gently," Tatiana said to Walter.

Walter slid a hand under Elliot's shoulders and lifted him up a few inches.

"Pour," Tatiana said to Whitey. She was in charge for the moment.

Whitey filled the shot glass and handed it to her. She managed, somehow, with her slender finger, to pry apart Elliot's clenched teeth. She poured the brandy into his mouth, three little swallows. The wounded man choked on the last one. Walter lowered his head back down onto the pillow. After a moment, the wounded man's eyelids fluttered and a little moan of pain escaped him.

Walter made happy sounds, gesturing.

Breslin and Whitey moved in closer. Jones stood by the door, scowling, playing with his gun. At last Elliot opened his eyes and looked up into Tatiana's pale, lovely face. He was obviously lost for the moment.

"Elliot!" Breslin said.

Elliot turned his head and made a little grimace of pain. He saw his man, and his world came back into focus. His bluish lips moved.

"Bad?" he whispered.

"Real bad. Sorry," Breslin said.

"It's so bad, Mr. Elliot," Tatiana said, "that unless these people will send for a doctor you aren't going to make it."

Elliot turned his head again, and again it cost him. "You helping?"

"With much too limited skills, Mr. Elliot," she said.

"The cops haven't come back," Breslin said. "No sign of any trouble. You were right, I think. That trooper didn't tumble to anything. We can't call a local doctor without blowing everything. We thought we should drive you or fly you to the city. You know where to reach Dixon?"

"No," Elliot whispered.

"Then he won't be back until tomorrow. Too late. This guy Quist can fly a chopper, but it seems risky."

Elliot's lips moved in a ghastly smile. "Joke," he said.

"So it has to be by car," Breslin said.

"You won't make it, Mr. Elliot," Tatiana said quietly. "With that bullet in you, you won't make it."

There was a moment of silence. "Brandy," Elliot said.

Whitey filled another shot glass and this time, with Tatiana's help, Elliot drank from it. He coughed again, and a little fleck of blood appeared at the corner of his mouth.

"So you leave me here and make your own getaway," Elliot said to Breslin.

"And lose our cut?" Jones said from the doorway.

"The whole thing is screwed up," Elliot said, and closed his eyes. But the brandy was doing its work. Spots of color appeared on his cheeks.

"It's a doctor or else," Tatiana said.

"So we call a doctor," Elliot said. That grisly smile moved his lips again. "The rest of you stay out of sight. I was cleaning a gun—"

"And if the doctor doesn't buy that?" Breslin asked.

"Unfortunate for him," Elliot said, and turned his face away to hide a spasm of pain.

"We're supposed to be in touch with Feydhev this evening, aren't we?" Breslin asked. "How do we get you to an outside phone?"

"Maybe you do the talking, Bres," Elliot said. "Right now I don't give much of a damn about anything except this pain! There's a new young doctor in town. I think his name is Cross."

Before they got through with this, Quist thought, Elliot and his people would be stacking up bodies like cordwood. Their share of the payoff must be enormous. A young doctor, probably ready to make house calls in an emergency, would walk into this murder trap as innocently as a steer goes into a slaughterhouse. No way to stop him, no way to warn him.

Breslin left the room. Where were the telephones in this house, Quist wondered? The one chance for any of them, Tatiana, himself, the doctor, was to get to a phone and sound the alarm. He was conscious that as time dragged on he wasn't thinking seriously of a successful escape. His one dream was to find a way to reveal these people to the authorities while he was still able to act.

Eventually Breslin came back to the library.

"Dr. Cross is on his way," he said.

Elliot made what was an enormous effort for a man in his condition. "The doctor mustn't catch on that anything's wrong except this hole in my gut till after—" He paused, coughing. "Move these two out of here, well away. We don't want any screaming or yelling to distract Dr. Cross."

"Where?" Breslin asked.

"Up the mountain, back of the house," Elliot said. "Old marble quarry. There's an abandoned stonecutting shop up there. Jones and Whitey—take them up, stay with them."

"Look," Breslin said. "Sooner or later we're going to have to—" He found the words hard to say. "Why wait?"

"Because we may need to make one more tape for Feydhev, some kind of assurance."

"We'll weaken our force down here," Breslin said.

"We don't need an army to take care of one eager young doctor," Elliot said. He looked at Tatiana. "I'm sorry to seem ungracious, Miss Feydhev. Thanks for your help." He turned his head away. "Move them."

Once more, Jones clamped one end of the handcuffs over Quist's right wrist. He grabbed Tatiana, dragged her close, and fastened the other end over her left wrist.

"Walk!" he said.

CHAPTER FIVE

Dr. Norman Cross, thirtyish, fair skinned, with a pleasant, cheerful manner, had moved to the town of Waterford, Vermont, six months ago, after carefully planning his career. In an age of specialists, he was intrigued by the image of the old-fashioned country doctor. His grandfather had been one, a king figure in a small town. People had counted on old Dr. Cross, expected him to be available at any time of the day or night, expected him to come to them when they called, loved him and respected him. Young Dr. Cross wanted something like that for himself. People to people, something personal between doctor and patient, seemed more important to him in the art of healing than the highly technical and complex techniques of hospital care.

This very personal concept was about to threaten Dr. Norman Cross's life, although he had no idea of it when the call came to him in his office, which he maintained in his own home.

"I'm calling for Mr. Brooks Elliot, Doctor. The old Simmons place in the valley?" the voice on the phone said.

"I know where it is," Cross said.

"Mr. Elliot has had an accident. He was cleaning a gun—"

"Maybe we should get him to the hospital," Cross said.

"I'd appreciate it if you could come quickly, Doctor—

make your decision after you've seen Mr. Elliot. I'm afraid he needs help quickly."

"Take me ten, fifteen minutes," Cross said.

There was no thought in the doctor's mind of any sort of trap. Gunshot wounds were not the rarest kind of accident in the country, though this wasn't the time of year for hunters. But men who owned guns had a way of caring for them like children. Cleaning a gun was not a freakish occupation. "Damn fool should have known whether it was loaded," Dr. Cross told himself.

Dr. Cross was a bachelor. He hadn't yet developed a large enough practice to justify a permanent nurse during office hours. So it was that he left for the Elliot place without telling anyone, or leaving any kind of message. He had a mechanical answering service on his phone. "This is Dr. Cross speaking. I am not in my office now. If it is an emergency, call Dr. Barstow in Rutland. At the sound of the buzzer leave your name and telephone number. I'll get back to you. Thank you."

Dr. Cross went out to his car and was on his way to disappearing. He glanced at his watch as he headed down the main highway toward the old Simmons estate. The sun had disappeared, and out of dark clouds in the West came the rumble of thunder. It looked, he thought, as though they were about to have a whopper. Lightning suddenly streaked the sky. If he hadn't been in such a hurry when he left his house he would have noticed and remembered to bring his raincoat and a hat.

Heavy splotches of rain spotted the doctor's windshield as he turned off the highway and started down the bluestone driveway to the red brick house below. He was just going to make it, he thought, before the skies opened up for real. Thunder rumbled and sudden gusts of high wind whipped at the trees lining the driveway. It was almost as dark as night.

Dr. Cross drove as close to the front door as he could, picked up his medical bag and ran for it. He had just reached the cover of the overhang at the front door when the deluge came. The door opened as he reached for the brass knocker, and he lurched into the reception hall beyond.

"Wow, I could have been drowned," Cross said, wiping raindrops from his face with his handkerchief. He saw that the man who'd opened the door for him was black, wearing a white houseman's jacket. The man made some odd kind of noise and beckoned Cross to follow.

In the library, Cross saw his patient on the couch, midriff bare, a bloody cloth covering the wound in his stomach. Standing by the wounded patient was a grey-haired man in a business suit.

"My name is Smith," Breslin said. "I'm the one who called you, Doctor. Thanks for coming. Mr. Elliot is in a lot of pain."

Cross lifted the bloody cloth and made a whistling sound. "What the hell was he cleaning, a cannon?" He looked around, but he didn't see a gun anywhere.

Lightning seemed to strike just outside the window, and thunder literally shook the house.

"Too damn close for comfort," Breslin said. "You have storms like this often, Doctor?"

"Every time I go out without a raincoat," Cross said, and bent over his patient.

Elliot's eyes fluttered open. "Stupid carelessness," he whispered.

Cross took off his jacket and began rolling up his sleeves. "Bullet still in him?" he asked. "Didn't come out the other side?"

"No, Doctor. It's still in him."

"You better phone for that ambulance," Cross said. "Rutland Hospital."

Breslin hesitated, and then he walked out of the room, leaving Cross alone with his patient and the black man.

"How long ago did this happen?" Cross asked.

Walter made his inarticulate sounds, opened his mouth and pointed.

"Jesus!" Cross said. He leaned close to Elliot. "Pain bad?"

"Bad," Elliot said.

"I'm going to give you something for it," Cross said, opening his medical bag. "I'm going to have to probe around in there a little."

He prepared something in a hypodermic. Outside the storm threatened to tear the house apart. Cross rubbed Elliot's arm with cotton soaked in alcohol and stabbed it with the needle, pressing the plunger in slowly.

Breslin came back from wherever he'd gone. "That big crack must have knocked out the phone," he said. "Line's dead."

"Damn," Cross said. He put down the needle. "Take a few minutes for that to take hold. You got the gun he was shot with? I'd like to see what kind of a slug I'm looking for."

Breslin's face was an expressionless mask. "It happened outside," he said. He glanced at the windows, against which the rain was beating angrily. "It's probably still out there. We didn't think about it when we saw he was hurt."

Breslin knew where the gun was. It was in Jones's pocket, or in his hand. My God, he thought, climbing that mountain in this storm with two handcuffed prisoners was no picnic.

"Move one of those lamps over here," Dr. Cross said to Walter.

Walter moved one of the reading lamps and focused it directly over Elliot's wound. He turned the switch at the neck of the lamp and nothing happened. The storm had knocked out the electric power as well as the telephone.

"Wind probably blown some tree limbs down on the

lines," Cross said. He turned to Breslin. "I can't work on him in this light, Mr. Smith. I guess we'll have to get him into my car and take him to the hospital that way."

"Bleeding?" Breslin asked.

"I think I can stop the worst of it," Cross said. "You drive the car. I'll ride with Elliot in the back. You got a station wagon out there in that garage I saw? He could ride flat in a wagon."

"I'm afraid you're going to have to work on him here, Doctor," Breslin said.

There was another savage flash of lightning and earth-shaking thunder.

"What are you talking about?" Cross said, when he could make himself heard. "I can't do anything here safely. No light. God knows how long the power will be out." He looked around. "Something we can use as a stretcher to get him out to the car?"

"I'm sorry, Doctor, but it's going to have to be here," Breslin said in a silky, smooth voice.

Cross turned on him. "Now, listen to me—" He stopped. He was looking into the muzzle of a very competent-looking handgun.

"I'm sorry, Doctor. I hoped it wouldn't come to this."

Young Dr. Cross couldn't believe what he was seeing and hearing. "If this is some kind of joke—"

"No joke, Doctor."

"This man can die if he doesn't get the proper attention!"

"Then give him the proper attention," Devlin said.

Lightning struck close again, and the almost-instant thunder rattled the windows. Little beads of sweat had appeared on Dr. Cross's forehead. He had walked, wide open, into something he didn't understand; something obviously criminal. It hadn't occurred to him, yet, that the danger he faced was anything more than losing a patient because he had to treat him under adverse conditions.

"It's on your head," he said to Breslin. "You got any decent-size flashlights in the house? I've got to see what I'm doing."

CHAPTER SIX

Sam Walton's little apartment in Greenwich Village was arranged so that he never had to leave the big armchair in which he sat for hours at a time. His telephone was within reach. The remote control of his television set sat next to the phone on one table by his right hand. On another table, on the other side of the chair, was an electric coffee percolator and a blue china mug. He had no need to leave his chair except to go to the john, or twice a day when he made the monumental effort, gasping for breath, to go to the small kitchenette to prepare himself a meal. His life consisted of a permanent struggle for air.

Sam had received a call from his "source." He had written down a list of names on a pad he kept next to the coffeepot, along with a ball-point pen. He had talked for some time with his source, and the simple business of a lengthy conversation was exhausting. He had made the effort, however, to call his friend Lieutenant Kreevich. Kreevich was not at police headquarters nor at his own apartment. Sam left a message at headquarters, poured himself a cup of coffee, and leaned back in his chair to reorganize his strength. He saw, on the electric clock over his TV set, that it was just after six o'clock in the evening. Sam felt no particular urgency about the situation. He'd told Kreevich he might have something for him by the end of the day. The homicide man would call him when he got around to it. Sam sipped his coffee and switched on the TV to watch the on-going six o'clock news.

Kreevich, following his useless session with Rhaman Feydhev, had spent some time in the Trapeze Bar at the Beaumont with one of his men, who was still combing the area for some witness to the kidnapping who hadn't come forward for some reason. Routine effort to identify the car used by the kidnappers was pretty hopeless after two and a half days. Kreevich felt, with some frustrated bitterness, that he was caught in a familiar after-the-fact rat race. While he looked for small clues to give him some kind of lead, Quist and Feydhev's daughter might already have run out of time. He was where he always found himself, not preventing a crime but trying to solve it after it was committed.

It was about a quarter to seven when he broke up with his man and went to a pay phone in the lobby of the hotel to call Sam Walton.

"Well, I've got something for you," Sam wheezed over the phone, "but I don't know how much good it is."

"Try me," Kreevich said.

"You got something to write on?"

Kreevich took a small notebook out of his pocket and put it on the shelf under the telephone. "Shoot," he said.

"There is a list of reasonably competent hit men as long as from here to there," Sam said. "You can take 'em down if you want, but you better be sitting. However, my source thinks none of those people is big enough to handle the kind of operation you've got. He came up with four names he thinks might handle a multimillion-dollar scoop."

"Let's have them," Kreevich said.

"There's a man named Lucien Zachery in San Francisco."

"Address?"

"I don't have an address for him or the others," Sam said.

"Just a locality. Probably local police could help. They're not unknown, they're just not in jail. If you're good, you don't wind up with a record or under surveillance."

"Go ahead."

"There's a man named Paul Davis, in Detroit," Sam said. "He was suspected of being back of the hijacking of a plane to Cuba a year ago; a hundred and some passengers held hostage. Half a dozen men on the job. One of them was caught and was known to be a friend of Davis's. He wouldn't talk, and Davis was at home reading the funnies when the hijacking took place. He's big league, though."

"Next," Kreevich said.

"There's an Igor Teliski, Washington, D.C. He's my choice, if its one of the four, Mark. Polish-American, but very clubby with the Arab lobby in Washington. My source thinks he's pulled some very fancy capers for the big oil people in the Middle East. Interpol has him marked down as the kidnapper of Benito Castellano, the Italian millionaire. Five million bucks changed hands there, but they were never able to nail Teliski for it. Like I said, the good ones don't get nailed."

"And number four?" Kreevich asked.

"Right here in this town. That may lean you toward him; knows the city, probably knows the surrounding countryside. His name is Brooks Elliot, and there have been rumors that he—"

"Say that name again!" Kreevich said, his muscles tightening.

"Brooks Elliot."

"That's it, Sam. I didn't tell you, I guess, but my man Quist was forced to make a tape for the kidnappers. He said something on it that set us looking for a man named Elliot to whom we thought he was referring. It wasn't that Elliot. It was *this* Elliot! No definite address?"

"I told you. But it's your city, Mark. Good luck."

Kreevich could feel his heart beating a little faster. The first thing he did was look in the phone book. It couldn't be that simple, but it was worth a try.

It wasn't that simple.

Twenty minutes later he was in his office with a staff of people working for him. Did anyone named Brooks Elliot have a criminal record? He called Agent Rubek. Did the FBI have anything on a Brooks Elliot? He had a contact in the CIA. Same question. The IRS—if the man had ever filed a tax return under that name there would be an address. Computers work fast in this day and age. Kreevich came up with a zero in all four places.

Sam had warned him. The good ones don't get caught.

He called Sam back and told him what he had done and that he had come up empty. "Your source named him, Sam. How would he know?"

"This is a world of whispers," Sam said. "If you live in it you hear things. Like me."

"Can I talk to your source?"

"Sorry, Mark."

"Just on the telephone? Without knowing who he is? If your source knows his name he might know where he hangs out, what other names he uses."

"Can't do it, Mark. Rules of the game. But I'll talk to him again."

"Make it quick, friend. A couple of lives may depend on it."

Kreevich kept at it while he waited to hear from Sam again. He called Sergeant Stryker at Lake Toromog. Did anyone there know a Brooks Elliot? Kreevich had heard from Dan Garvey about his trip to Philadelphia. He tried there. Did the name Brooks Elliot mean anything to Joey Mandel or Cannikin? No dice.

His final thought had to do with the helicopter. It had to be registered, licensed somewhere. The word went out on police lines to hundreds of airports, large and small, within two hundred miles of Lake Toromog.

Kreevich leaned back in his office chair, opening a fresh pack of cigarettes. There was nothing to do now but wait. He'd had one piece of luck. He needed just one more.

A world of whispers, Sam had called it. Kreevich brought his fist down on his desk. "Goddamn it, let someone speak out loud, just for once!"

CHAPTER SEVEN

Quist and Tatiana, linked together by the steel cuffs, were hustled out a rear door of the house and into the garden Quist had seen from his second-floor window. Jones and Whitey were directly behind them. Whitey had acquired the machine pistol Quist had seen in the possession of one of the garden guards earlier. Jones, he knew without seeing, had that deadly .44 he was so quick to use. There was a pause in the garden to talk to the two guards there. Whitey told them they were to stay out of sight, but to be ready if Breslin needed them.

"If this doctor that's coming gets nosey—" Whitey said.

"You know where this damn quarry is up the mountain?" Jones asked. "There's some kind of a building up there, Elliot says."

"Old stonecutting mill," the garden man said. "Elliot had me look it over while you were in New York. Said we might have to use it."

"Well, where the hell is it? We got to move, man."

"More reason than the doctor," the garden man said. He was looking up at the black sky in the west. "If that storm hits before you get there, you'll need a boat."

"Damn!" Jones said. "Why us?"

The garden guard explained that there was an old work road that led to the quarry and the abandoned mill. "But it comes in off the main highway, way north of here. You'll be seen if you go along the flat land to find it. Best thing is to go straight into the woods there and start climbing up. You should hit the road about halfway to the quarry. As long as you keep going up you can't miss it."

The first distant rumble of thunder reached them.

"So move, pals," Jones said.

Quist felt the barrel of the .44 rammed into his back. He looked to the west and saw a sliver of lightning in the sky. The mountain ahead of them had a bright patch of sunlight at its dark-green summit.

Tatiana had managed to link her fingers in his. It would keep them from tugging at each other with the handcuff. It gave her some kind of comfort and reassurance.

The thunder came closer as the sky darkened all around them.

The first hundred yards were across a mowed field, the footing easy. Jones kept urging them to move faster. It was late afternoon, but it seemed that night was closing in on them. Tatiana stumbled, but Quist managed to keep her from falling. Something that sounded like a little gasping sob came from her.

The lightning and the thunder came again, close together. Quist remembered that as a kid he'd been told that if you counted, slowly, between the lightning and the thunder you could tell how many miles away the storm was. There was barely time for a count of one now.

Quist had waited and waited for the right moment to make any sort of move that was left to him, and he had waited too long. Anchored to Tatiana, they were like kids in a three-legged race, each unable to function without the cooperation of the other. A couple of miles, someone had said, to the abandoned mill. And when they got there, Quist thought, their chances of ever leaving it were very slight. They were only alive now because there was still a chance they might be needed to make another tape. They could refuse, and die knowing they'd made it difficult for the enemy. They could do what they were told, and because they were human there would always seem to be hope until the very last second, till Jones's finger tightened on the trigger of his .44.

"Not good enough!" Quist told himself. There had to be something positive, some last effort, no matter how far out. But what, where, and how?

A sudden gust of wind set them to staggering as they approached the thick woods at the foot of the mountain. Several isolated raindrops splashed Quist's face. The storm seemed, by some miracle, to have passed over them and to be waiting for them in the woods ahead. A jagged streak of lightning struck a tree not ten yards away, splitting it, leaving its naked flesh revealed. The thunder rocked them, and Quist and Tatiana instinctively stumbled back into Jones and Whitey. The two men were swearing.

"God, that was right on top of us!" Whitey said.

Then the deluge.

It wasn't like rain. It seemed as if someone was pouring buckets of water on them from above. In seconds they were soaked to the skin, hair matted, unable to see six feet in front of them. All around them was the lightning and thunder, the noise almost unbearable.

"I say we go back!" Whitey shouted.

"No way," Jones shouted back. "Just as far one way as the other. Get moving, Quist!"

No one in his right mind was meant to make this climb up through the woods. The brush was thick; you had to fight your way through it. The gusts of wind blew low-hanging tree limbs against their bodies, into their faces. Every muscle in Quist's body ached from the effort, and he could feel Tatiana begin to drag behind.

Quist stopped and turned. Through the torrential rain, Jones and Whitey were blurred figures.

"Why don't we just stay put till this passes?" Quist shouted. "We're out of sight of the house."

"There's shelter up ahead somewhere," Jones shouted back. "Keep moving! We could get killed in here."

They struggled on a few yards and seemed to come face to face with a blank wall of rock and shrubs. It rose up out of sight in the rain.

"Go left!" Jones shouted. "We got to find our way around it and keep on up. That goddamn road has to be somewhere."

They moved to the left. The face of what was a cliff evaporated. They struggled up. Tatiana kept going down to her knees, and Quist would lift her as gently as he could and pull her on, still holding her hand.

It seemed to take forever to reach what appeared to be level ground again. It was a fairly clear patch stretching along the top of the cliff they had just skirted. The rain beat at them almost cruelly. Quist stopped, gasping for breath. He turned and put his left arm around Tatiana, holding her close. She was crying.

"I can't go any farther, Julian. I just can't!"

Looking back, Quist saw that they'd opened quite a gap between themselves and Jones and Whitey. Whitey was crawling the last yards on his hands and knees. Jones, an arm raised to shield his face against the driving rain, was swearing methodically, almost rhythmically.

Quist lowered his head and spoke into Tatiana's ear. "We

don't have a chance, luv, except to make a chance," he said. "Thousand to one against us. You willing?"

She looked up, eyes squinted against the rain, and nodded.

"Hold on," Quist said.

His left arm tightened around her and he lurched toward the edge of the cliff. They went over the edge like two lovers locked in a suicidal death leap. Jones's shout and the sound of his gun firing were drowned out by a bolt of lightning that struck a tree only a few feet away and the deafening roar of thunder that went with it. Jones knelt on the edge of the cliff, his gun moving from side to side, searching for a target. Whitey, still crawling, finally lay flat on his stomach looking down. There was nothing to be heard over the storm. From down below a kind of thick mist, created by the torrents of rain, rose up toward them. There was no way to see anything beyond the reach of your hand.

At the foot of the cliff Quist lay, half stunned, his arms still around a motionless Tatiana. They had bounced and rolled over rocks and bushes for what seemed like forever. When the fall ended they were caught in the stubborn arms of an evergreen shrub of some sort. Around them the storm raged, the rain pelted down on them.

Very tentatively, Quist tried moving his legs and then his arms. Everything hurt, but everything seemed to work. He moved, straddling Tatiana on his hands and knees, shielding her upturned face from the rain with his body. With his free hand he managed to get a handkerchief out of his pocket. It was soaking wet, but he used it to wipe the girl's matted hair off her forehead and eyes. Her eyelids moved and she looked up at him.

"You all in one piece?" He was shouting at her, but no one could hear.

"My God, Julian!" she said.

She tried her legs. She was still wearing the taffeta dinner dress she'd had on the night of the kidnapping. It was ripped and torn, caked with dirt like the patches of bare skin that were revealed. Her stockings were in shreds. She had lost a shoe somewhere in the fall.

She gave him a crooked little smile. "I must look a fright," she said.

"How you look doesn't matter, luv. Can you move?"

"I—I think so."

"Because we've got to get away from this spot as fast and as far as we can." He looked up. He couldn't see the top of the cliff through the haze and the rain. But one thing was certain. Jones and Whitey were already on the way down.

Lightning struck again and the thunder beat at them. Quist lifted Tatiana to a standing position.

"Better kick off that other shoe," he said.

"But Julian—walking barefoot through this stuff!"

"You want to live, don't you, Tatiana? It was a thousand to one at the top of the cliff. It's five hundred to one now, but you have to take it as it comes, baby."

Clinging to each other, they scrambled away from the cliff face. A stabbing pain in his side suggested to Quist that he had bruised or broken ribs. It was like night in the woods except for the jagged streaks of lightning. Quist, a step ahead of the girl, held his left forearm in front of his face as a shield against brush and tree limbs. Occasionally they had to get down on their knees to crawl under an obstruction. He sensed that, for all her courage, the girl wasn't going to be able to travel much farther. He was hoping to find a dense patch of brush, the miracle of overhanging rocks under which they could hide. If they could stay hidden for an hour or so, while Jones and Whitey thrashed around in the gloom, the cover of real night darkness would come to their aid, even when this storm had spent itself.

He stumbled and fell, down into a little punchbowl declivity, dragging Tatiana, inadvertently, down on top of him. The handcuff tore at the flesh on his forearm and he heard a little cry of pain from Tatiana. She lay on top of him, weeping softly.

A garish streak of lightning showed him for an instant where they were. A giant tree, struck in the storm, had toppled over, uprooting itself. They had fallen into the hole left by those ripped-up roots. The roots, like a mass of crooked arms, made a barrier on one side of the hole. Thick masses of brush surrounded the other sides. It was in breaking through that brush that Quist had stumbled down into the hole he couldn't see, dragging Tatiana with him.

He managed to move her, gently, and sit up. His head was just above the ground level of the surrounding forest. He was sitting, he realized, in water, which was pouring into the hole from a self-made little drainage ditch at one side.

"This is it," he told Tatiana. "If you can move just a little bit more, my luv, we can sit with our backs against those roots. They'll protect us from one side."

She didn't say anything but she made the effort. They were finally sitting side by side, pressed closely together, leaning back against the wall of roots. Quist saw lightning up through the treetops, but it was a good count of four before he heard the thunder. The rain still pelted down.

"It's passing on," he said.

"Then what?" Tatiana said.

"They have to find us," Quist said. "In the dark, I hope. I don't think either one of them is a boy scout."

They sat there, pressed together, straining to hear something they knew they couldn't hear over the retreating storm. Quist remembered some old school-day's question: Is there really noise when there is nobody to hear it? Had there been shots as they went tumbling down the cliff? The storm at its height had obliterated that sound. He could imagine Jones and Whitey backtracking down the trail they'd climbed, to get to the bottom of the cliff. He could imagine little rock slides, as they dug in their heels to keep from falling. No one to hear those. He could almost see the wind slashing rain into their faces, see them fighting to orient themselves, trying to guess just where Quist and Tatiana might have landed after their leap into space. There would be no trail to follow, thanks to the torrential rain. They would stumble around, almost as blind and hopeless as Quist and Tatiana had been.

The rain was easing up. Looking up through the trees, Quist could see the faint grey of twilight. He wasn't a praying man, but in his own way he prayed. Separate and free, he and Tatiana might have had a chance to run for it, to maneuver away from a search, but anchored together by these unrelenting handcuffs they couldn't travel anymore for now. There was no way on earth to defend themselves against an attack if it came. They were sitting ducks. He could imagine Jones, standing on the rim of their little hole, smiling at them and pumping lead into them from his .44. Twenty years from now some adventurous kid might find their bleached bones here in the woods.

And then it happened. Jones was not ten feet away from them, shouting at Whitey. Quist reached across and covered Tatiana's mouth with his hand.

"No sign of them!" Jones shouted.

They could hear Whitey's voice, but not what he was saying. There was still too much noise from the storm.

"There's probably five million acres of these goddamn woods," Jones said. "Be pitch dark in another hour. Maybe you ought to go back to the house and get some flashlights."

Still Whitey's response was garbled.

"You think you can find me here? No point in moving around until we can see what we're doing."

More voice without words.

"I'll be somewhere near the base of that cliff—unless I hear something. They can't stay in one place forever."

That's just what they were going to have to do, Quist thought. He couldn't tell whether Jones moved away or whether he stayed where he was, just a few yards away. They waited, waited, waited. Finally Quist could feel Tatiana stirring under his hand. He took it away from her mouth. They stared at each other in the darkness, not really seeing each other. They didn't dare speak. The rain had subsided, but water dripping from the trees made considerable noise.

The light in the sky had died out and it was night.

Suddenly Tatiana's free hand reached up and went around Quist's neck, her lips at his ear.

"I don't want to just wait here to die, Julian," she whispered.

What could he offer her? What could he promise her? The marines?

CHAPTER EIGHT

Kreevich sat in his office at police headquarters in New York, waiting for a miracle. The FBI had come up with nothing on a Brooks Elliot. The CIA had nothing on such a man. His own records at headquarters were blank. His best bet, he had dreamed, was the Internal Revenue Service. You don't live in this country without making a tax return. But Brooks Elliot hadn't made one. The computers were full of millions of names, but "Brooks Elliot" refused to surface. The last resort left to him was the airports, where a helicopter might be registered in the owner's name. Kreevich wasn't hopeful. A man who kept his name so carefully off all records was unlikely to let his foot slip in this area. Quist had tried to tell him something on the tape, but what had seemed a bright hope, when Sam Walton reported, was fading.

A crisp-looking young policewoman came into Kreevich's office. She was Sergeant Duane. She had worked with Kreevich on another case that had involved Julian Quist, and she knew how much the lieutenant cared for his friend.

"Coffee?" she asked.

"What I need is a triple bourbon and three days' sleep," Kreevich said.

"I can get you the bourbon," Sergeant Duane said.

She was too damn pretty, Kreevich thought, to be involved with crime. He often kidded her about the word "policewoman." Should he call her a "policeperson" in this day of women's lib?

"Coffee will have to do, Sergeant," he said. "Thanks."

"These reports from the airports, especially the small ones, are slow coming in," she said. "There isn't any master computer to store their information, like the FBI or the other big ones have."

"I know," Kreevich said.

He sat, staring straight ahead. Machines, computers, records produced nothing. Once more around the clock to morning and Feydhev would have run out of time. Feydhev was going to say "no" to the kidnappers demands, and that would be the end for his daughter and for Quist. Once around the clock, and all the scientific aids did nothing to help. He had a vision of police working the airports, using dogs to smell out smuggled drugs. He needed a dog with a nose for kidnappers, he thought. He would take the dog to Lake Toromog, set him on the trail at Cannikin's cabin, and the dog would walk fifteen yards out of the house, pause, and look up into the sky. That's how far a nose for kidnapping would take him. He had been there himself, for three days, in effect staring up into an empty sky.

Sergeant Duane came back with coffee in a mug. She put it down in front of Kreevich. She had some papers in her hand and was frowning at them.

"I keep going over these reports from some of the small airports, Lieutenant. This one came in some hours ago from a place in Vermont, Waterford. They have seven choppers in the area and they checked them all out. All accounted for at the critical time. Every time I go to put it aside something stops me."

"Hunch?" Kreevich asked. He believed in his own hunches but doubted anyone else's.

"I don't know, Lieutenant. It rings some kind of a bell, but I don't know what bell. Maybe you'll see something I'm missing."

Kreevich glanced at the report. It had been phoned in by a Sergeant Norris at the Waterford State Police barracks in Waterford, Vermont. It was a list of seven names and addresses, all present and accounted for, in effect. Routine jobs, routinely done. There was no Brooks Elliot on the list for sure. Duane wouldn't have needed a hunch to pick that up.

He went down the list of seven names, which told him nothing the first time around. The name at the very bottom was "George Dixon." The address was "Oblong Valley House." Kreevich felt his muscles go tense.

"Sergeant, sergeant, sergeant!" he said.

"You spot something, sir?"

"Kid at Lake Toromog, Jerry Tinker. You saw the report on him?"

"Yes, sir. He heard the shot that killed the dog."

"Right. And he had a CB radio, and he heard the helicopter pilot talking to someone. Remember what he heard?"

"Some kind of code signal they weren't able to trace."

"Think, Sergeant. Because that's what your hunch is all about."

Her wide blue eyes widened. "Oblong Courier, right?"

"Right, by God! Name of the place where this Dixon, who owns a chopper, lives. Oblong Valley House—Oblong Courier."

"Oh, wow!" Sergeant Duane said.

"See if you can get me this Sergeant Norris at the Waterford barracks," Kreevich said. "I'll talk to anyone else there if he's not on duty."

Sergeant Duane picked up the phone on Kreevich's desk. She got the number she wanted through information and dialed it. Eventually she turned to Kreevich. "They've had some kind of massive electrical storm up there," she reported. "Power and telephone lines down."

"Get the next nearest barracks—Rutland, wherever."

A few minutes later Kreevich was talking to the trooper in charge at the Rutland barracks.

"I'm not familiar with the names of properties down there," the trooper said. "Everybody's got a name for their houses. That's what Oblong Valley House sounds like. I know it's not a hotel or a motel."

"It's a shot in the dark," Kreevich said. "You've heard about the Feydhev kidnapping and the abduction of a man named Quist?"

"It was on television, while we still had television," the trooper said. "All hell broke out here in the late afternoon. Biggest damn electrical storm I ever saw. Trees down, wires down. That's why you couldn't reach the Waterford barracks."

"It's just possible that the kidnappers are holed up in this Oblong Valley House place," Kreevich said. "I'd like it covered, surrounded."

"I'll have to get authority from Captain Stevens, if I can

find him," the trooper said. "Everybody's out on the roads, because of the storm."

"I don't want him to go in," Kreevich said sharply. "Just see that nobody leaves. Try to barge in and the people I'm concerned about could be shot dead in their tracks. How long will it take me to drive up there?"

"Three hours and a half if you step on it."

"I'm stepping on it. Try to have this Sergeant Norris, who knows the area, available."

"Do my best, Lieutenant."

"Tell your Captain Stevens I'll see he gets a medal provided he just contains whoever's at this Oblong Valley place. Tell him if he gets eager, moves in, and get my people shot, I'll cut out his heart."

The trooper chuckled. "I'll tell him something, Lieutenant."

Kreevich put down the phone and turned to Sergeant Duane. "I want an unmarked police car for a long-distance run," he said. "I'll be down front in ten minutes."

"Yes, sir."

"And, Sergeant?"

"Yes, sir?"

"If you turn out to have been right about this, when I get back I might buy you a Rolls-Royce, or make love to you till your ears light up. Anything you ask."

A faint color rose in Sergeant Duane's cheeks. "I just might take you up on that, sir," she said, and was gone.

Kreevich dialed a number. Lydia Morton answered on the second ring.

"It's Mark, Lydia. Mark Kreevich."

"What other Mark?" she said. "Is there—?"

"Something, we hope," Kreevich said. "A lead to where they might be held."

"Where?"

"To hell and gone up in Vermont. You remember the helicopter signal the Tinker kid heard on his CB radio?"

"Oblong Courier," Lydia said.

"Good girl," Kreevich said. "Well, a man who owns a chopper lives in a place called Oblong Valley House. It could be a wild coincidence. My bones tell me something else. Stay hopeful, Lydia."

"Can I go with you?"

"I wish I thought it made sense to say yes," Kreevich said. "I'll be in touch just as soon as I have anything to report."

Outside headquarters a sleek black Imperial waited for Kreevich. Sergeant Duane was standing beside it.

"I've drawn you a trip map, Lieutenant," she said. "Terminal at the Waterford barracks or the Rutland barracks, whichever you decide."

Kreevich grinned at her. "I might even marry you, Sergeant," he said.

He got in behind the wheel. Three and a half hours away there could be answers.

There is a terrible monotony to driving distances at night. It was just about ten o'clock when Kreevich started his strip. The early part of it was along parkways he knew well, and there was still considerable traffic going in and out of the city. He had to concentrate on his driving. But as midnight approached he found himself streaking through small towns that had already gone to bed, almost nothing coming the other way. His hopes were up, his adrenalin pumping, but staring mile after mile into the cone of light from his car had a mesmerizing affect. He was stopped twice by patrolling state troopers, once as he came off the thruway into New York State, and once somewhere near Pittsfield, Massachusetts. He was almost grateful for a break in the pattern.

It was just after one-thirty when he spotted the Waterford barracks. The trooper at the desk told him that Sergeant

Norris and Captain Stevens from Rutland were waiting for him. There's something look-alike about troopers in uniform; Kreevich thought he had seen these men or their counterparts many times before.

"We've had quite a day here," Sergeant Norris said, after the exchange of greetings. "Something like a tornado hit us in the late afternoon, power and phone lines down, trees uprooted, limbs down, freak accidents, and a local doctor missing. We've been trying to find him between emergencies. Then you call!"

Kreevich explained again what had brought him; the coincidence of the call signal from the chopper they thought had evacuated the kidnappers and their two hostages from Lake Toromog—"Oblong Courier"—and the discovery, almost by accident, that someone who owned a chopper here in Waterford lived in a place called Oblong Valley House.

"If that connection is real—the call signal and the name of the place where a chopper is kept—then it's entirely possible that the kidnappers and their hostages are at that house."

"So we go and ask," Captain Stevens said. He didn't suggest politely.

"There are millions of dollars at stake and two lives," Kreevich said. "If we go in openly, the kind of people involved will blow our heads off before we can knock on the front door. They don't mean to be caught, Captain."

"If they're there," the trooper captain said. "It could be a coincidence."

"If you believe in coincidences, Captain. I tend not to." Kreevich turned to Sergeant Norris. "What do you know about this fellow Dixon?"

"Not much. Wouldn't know him if I saw him," Norris said. "I was out there early yesterday, following up on the FBI request that we check on choppers. Dixon wasn't there, but I talked to the fellow he pilots for. I got the notion Dixon owns the chopper and rents it, and himself along with it, to this guy Elliot."

"This guy *who?*" Kreevich almost shouted.

"Brooks Elliot. He bought the Simmons place a couple of years ago. Didn't change the name old man Simmons gave it. Oblong Valley House."

"Bingo!" Kreevich said.

CHAPTER NINE

The woods were quiet now, except for the occasional sound of water dripping from the trees. Water was creating another problem for Quist and Tatiana. The little river was still running down into the hole, created by the uprooted tree, where they crouched. They were sitting waist deep in muddy water. Night had cooled things off, and, soaking wet, they clung to each other to generate some kind of heat.

They didn't dare move, didn't dare talk. They could hear Jones moving around not too far away. After what seemed an age, Whitey returned and there were two torches searching the woods. The two gunmen didn't move too far away from the cliff. One of them would stay put, and the other would move in ever-widening circles out from the spot where they felt Quist and Tatiana had landed after their first jump from the top. Sooner or later, Quist knew, one of them would very likely stumble on this hole where they were hiding. Now and then the two men called out to each other.

"Anything where you are, Whitey?"

"Nothing so far."

They didn't have to conceal their presence. The people they were looking for weren't armed. They couldn't move quickly, locked together by the handcuffs. The search was tedious, but it had to succeed in the end.

Whitey was moving closer now. Quist could see the light of his torch through the brush at the top of the hole. Quist made sign-language gestures to Tatiana. He moved away from the protection of the wall of roots, to the front edge of the hole. Standing upright, the water was rib high there, yet Quist's line of vision was just above ground level. He heard a little whimpering sound from Tatiana. Whitey's torch was only a few feet away, moving in an arc. Suddenly the blond gunman stepped forward and there he was, his light focused down on Quist and Tatiana. His machine pistol was aimed straight at them.

"Hey, you two look like a couple of drowned rats," he said. He turned his head to call out to Jones. The sound never developed because Quist reached out with his free hand and grabbed the man's ankle. He wrenched it with all the strength he had, and Whitey came tumbling down into the hole with a splashing noise.

"You okay, Whitey?" Jones called out from a distance away.

In all his life Quist had never prayed so hard for strength. With only one free hand he pushed down on Whitey, managed to straddle him so that his own weight was added. Tatiana, realizing what was happening, tried to maneuver so that Quist could use his right hand. Whitey tried to heave up, but Quist managed to hold his head under water. Quist felt sick at the thought of the muddy slime that Whitey had to be sucking into his lungs. But it was his life or theirs. It was a desperate struggle, quite suddenly all over.

Quist leaned against the wall of roots, gasping for breath.

Tatiana, an arm around him, rested her head against his shoulder, stifling the sound of spasmodic sobbing.

"Whitey, where are you, for God sake?" Jones seemed to be calling from the same distance away.

Quist began to search underwater and finally came up with Whitey's machine pistol. It was caked with mud. Whitey, or Quist himself, must have ground it into the earth in the fight.

"No chance the damn thing will work," Quist said.

He and Tatiana stared at each other.

"Our one chance, luv, is to make Jones think that it will," Quist said. "Stay close to me—as if you had any choice!"

CHAPTER TEN

A world of whispers, Sam Walton had called it. Brooks Elliot, whoever he was, had kept his name out of the major computers, but someone had whispered it to Sam Walton and Sam had whispered to Kreevich. Dixon, the pilot, had used a call name at Lake Toromog, perhaps improvised on the spot in an emergency, and an adolescent boy had heard it. And Quist, bless him, had provided them with a name on that tape, which Elliot himself must have edited. Quist had whispered and Elliot hadn't heard it.

Going over all this with Captain Stevens and Sergeant Norris, Kreevich had them convinced. His next move was to telephone Agent Frank Rubek. The FBI man wasn't at two different numbers Kreevich had. Another agent took a message for him.

"Tell him to call the state trooper barracks in Waterford, Vermont. I won't be here but someone will bring him up to date. Tell him we think we've located Brooks Elliot."

Tactics. Kreevich glanced at his watch. Two-thirty. Unless they'd tipped their hand in some fashion, things should be all quiet at Oblong Valley House. They would obviously be waiting for Feydhev to produce—or not produce—in the morning. That was the deadline.

Kreevich had a vision of Tatiana and Quist waiting under a gun, heavily guarded. Elliot might have some last-minute use for them before he eliminated them permanently. Kreevich had no doubt that Elliot would do just that; kill his hostages when they were no longer useful.

Wait till daylight when they could see what they were doing, was Captain Stevens's notion.

"How many men do you want to lose, Captain?" Kreevich argued. Time was running down while they talked. "That place must be an arsenal. God knows how many armed men are there. Walk in in daylight and they'll start shooting for their own lives. All they have to do is see us coming and the two hostages will be wiped out. I tell you our best bet is to go in with not too many men and catch them off guard, while it's still dark."

"I can have an army here in an hour or so," Stevens said.

"Either of you know what time it gets light?"

"A little before five," Norris said.

"We've got just about two hours," Kreevich said.

Stevens was a stubborn man. He was willing to go in with a few men while it was still dark, but he wanted his "army" in reserve. If anything went wrong in the first move, he'd have backup strength.

It took the captain twenty minutes to make calls. It would take another forty-five minutes to an hour for his force to assemble. They'd have less than an hour of darkness when the time came to strike. Kreevich couldn't overrule the captain. He had no authority here in Waterford. All he could do was wait—and sweat.

Sergeant Norris was of some use. He was able to draw them a reasonably detailed map of the grounds, the house, the hangar for the chopper, the barns where the power tools were kept. He and Kreevich were able to devise a plan of attack while Captain Stevens summoned his backup force. They couldn't risk the headlights of cars anywhere near the house. They'd have to go in on foot.

They would split up and take three ways in. One group would go straight down the driveway to the front door of the house. Two other groups would cut across the property from either side. A couple of other men would quickly cover the hangar, the barns. If there was any kind of sentry, he might take cover in those outbuildings.

Finally, Stevens was ready to move. There were a dozen men, including Kreevich, Stevens, and Norris. They drove in three cars down the highway toward Oblong Valley House. One car drove past the entrance and parked just around a curve, invisible from the house. The middle car, containing Kreevich, Norris, and a trooper named Fisher, pulled into the road leading to an old sandbank where highway crews got sand for the roads during winter snowstorms. The third car stopped well up the line from the entrance.

Kreevich and his two men walked back to the main road and waited. There was to be a flash signal from Stevens when the flanking groups were in place.

"Just in case we're spotted, there's no point in making it easy for them," Kreevich said. "There are trees and shrubs along the drive?"

"Till you get to the little circle at the front door," Norris said.

"Use as much cover as we can," Kreevich said.

A flashlight blinked to the north of them and was answered by one to the south. Norris answered with his own torch and they were under way.

" 'Into the valley of death rode the six hundred,' " Kreevich said under his breath.

"How's that?" Norris whispered back.

"Nothing," Kreevich said.

They moved in the grass at the side of the road to avoid the sound of their shoes on the bluestone drive. A single light showed from a ground-floor window of the house as they approached. All asleep, or all waiting in the dark at the ready.

Kreevich ducked down behind a lilac bush, waiting for the two others to come up level with him. He realized he was breathing harder than his exertion demanded. He had been here before, approaching guns behind doors and windows that revealed nothing. It didn't occur to him not to be afraid. It had been agreed upon in advance that, if they reached the front door without incident, they would wait for flashlight signals from the flankers and then they would smash their way in. Once inside, seconds could mean the difference between life and death for the hostages.

They reached the little turnaround circle in front of the house. The next thirty yards to the front door were without any cover at all. Norris was at Kreevich's elbow.

"This is it," the sergeant said.

"Good luck," Kreevich said. He slipped his gun out of the shoulder holster he was wearing, took a deep breath, and, bent low, he ran across the grass for the front door, Norris behind him.

It was a miracle he hadn't really expected. No gunfire. No indication that anyone had seen them. Off to the right a flashlight blinked. There was an answer to the left. Norris stepped forward and with his heavy service revolver he shot at the door lock. Kreevich jammed his shoulder against the door and stumbled into the reception hall beyond. The single light they'd seen was burning on a small table.

There was suddenly a babble of sound as the flanking groups smashed windows to make their entrances from either side of the building.

There was no response of any kind from inside the house. Kreevich ripped open the door of a side room, found a light switch just inside, and revealed a comfortable-looking library. No one there. He turned back and saw someone halfway down the stairs from the second floor. It was a black man, hands raised in a gesture of frightened surrender.

Norris ran up the stairs, slapped the man over for a weapon, and shouted at him. "Where are they?"

The black man, Kreevich noticed, was fully dressed. He hadn't been sleeping, it seemed. He made strange, gargling, frightened noises. He opened his mouth wide and pointed with a shaking forefinger.

"Jesus," Norris shouted. "He hasn't got any tongue!"

Norris dragged Walter down the stairs to stand him beside Kreevich.

"Can you write?" Kreevich asked.

Walter nodded vigorously, waving toward the open library door. Norris pulled him in there, and in the drawer of the reading table Walter found a pad and a pencil. He scrawled something with a shaking hand.

"*Mr. Elliot has gone to New York,*" Walter wrote.

"And the others?" Kreevich asked.

Walter made frantic gestures, disclaiming any knowledge.

The flanking forces were crowding into the library now.

"Cover every inch of this place, cellar to attic," Captain Stevens ordered. His men scattered.

Kreevich stayed with Walter. "Where is the girl?"

Walter shook his head, looking bewildered.

"Quist?"

Another headshake.

"Write, Goddamn it!" Kreevich ordered.

Walter wrote again. *Mr. Elliot has gone to New York.*

Stevens's men searched the house, floor to floor, room to room. They searched the outbuildings, the garage, the hangar, the toolshed.

"Chopper there, cars there, nobody," was the report.

"This creep," Stevens said, pointing at Walter, "is the only person anywhere."

"Looks like they flew the coop," Norris said.

Stevens looked at Kreevich. "What next?" he asked.

Kreevich swore softly and at length under his breath. He didn't know what next.

CHAPTER ELEVEN

Quist pulled himself up the side of the hole, dragging Tatiana as gently as he could. The handcuff bit into his wrist. He knew it must be torturing her.

A little distance away Jones was shouting for Whitey, waving his torch. Whitey's dead body floated in the muddy hole, bulging eyes staring up at a dark sky that was beginning to show the very faint signs of dawn in the east.

There was no light at ground level. The heavy overhang of trees blotted out any signs of light. You could only see it if you looked straight up.

Clutching the useless machine pistol, Quist maneuvered himself and Tatiana behind a thick clump of bushes. Jones wasn't fifteen yards away, shouting for Whitey. Quist lowered his head and whispered to Tatiana.

"I'm going to try to bring him to us," he said. "Our only chance."

"Julian!"

"Do what we can," Quist said.

He kicked at some loose stones under his feet.

"That you, Whitey?" Jones shouted.

Quist made a low, moaning sound.

"You hurt, Whitey?"

Quist moaned again. Jones started forward, aiming his torch straight at the bushes.

"Why the hell don't you answer me, Whitey? You hurt?" There was a note of panic in the killer's voice, but he came straight on. He reached the bushes and Quist rose up, jamming the useless machine pistol into the man's stomach.

"My turn, buster," Quist said.

Jones was carrying his torch in his right hand, his .44 hanging down relaxed in his left. He glanced down at the machine pistol, dropped the torch and tried to shift the gun. Tatiana, her right hand free, grabbed for it. She had told Quist she'd been taught to defend herself. If she'd been seconds slower, it would have been all over. As it was the gun dropped into the leaves at Jones's feet. She was on it like a cat, had it pointed straight at Jones's head.

"If he makes a move, blow it off!" Quist said. With his free left hand he began to search Jones's pockets. He found what he was looking for, the key to the handcuffs.

They were free. Quist twisted Jones's hands behind his back and fastened them with the cuffs. Then he sat down on the grass and laughed. He would deny later that it was something close to hysteria.

But they weren't in the clear yet. They couldn't go back to the house, Quist thought. They must find the road that led to the old marble quarry and work their way out to the main highway. There they would flag someone down, get help.

Jones had no doubt what the .44 that Quist held in his back could do to him if he tried anything. He walked, and walked, and eventually they found the road. It took them in a wide circle away from the house, which they saw was brightly lighted on all floors.

At last they reached the highway. Coming from the south were the bright headlights of a car. It still wasn't light enough to do without them. Tatiana, looking like a ragged urchin, stood in the middle of the road, waving her arms.

The car slowed down and stopped, its headlights blinding them. A man got out from behind the wheel.

"What's wrong, ma'am?" the man asked. "I'm Sergeant Norris of the state police."

Someone behind the sergeant laughed, and Quist heard a voice he would have known anywhere in the world.

"Dr. Livingston, I presume."

And Kreevich stepped forward.

CHAPTER TWELVE

It seemed like centuries later. There had been phone calls from the barracks to everyone, to the FBI, to Rhaman Feydhev to tell him that his daughter was alive and safe, to Lydia and Dan Garvey from Quist, who refused to talk to anyone until those two calls were made.

Some of it was pieced together, although they could get nothing out of Jones and Walter, the only two they had in custody. Jones knew he was in the bag and was already looking forward to some kind of plea bargaining: the big fish in return for something less than the maximum. Quist and Tatiana could both testify they'd taken the .44 from him, and ballistics would tie him to the murder of Tatiana's escort the night of the kidnapping. Walter was something else again. The black man evidently felt some deep loyalty to Brooks Elliot, and nothing could be pried out of him.

The Waterford troopers now knew what had become of their missing Dr. Cross. He had been moved out, along with his patient and the rest of the guards and henchmen. Where to? New York, Walter had said, so it probably wasn't New York.

"If Cross manages to keep Elliot alive," Kreevich said, "the man may get generous and let him go. He may buy him off. We're spreading a net, but can we spread it wide enough? Elliot's had hours, and with his kind of connections he can be in Timbuctoo by now."

"So we've lost him," Captain Stevens said.

Kreevich's smile was grim. "My friend, Sam Walton, says we live in a world of whispers. They almost caught up with Elliot, those whispers. Maybe they will again."

Stevens approached Tatiana. "We have a car to take you back to your father, Miss Feydhev. There's no reason for you to go through any more of this."

She was sitting on a bench with Quist, her fingers locked in his. She lifted her mud-smeared face. "It will be as though we'd never met, Julian."

"Only if you want it that way," he said. He looked at Stevens. "Don't you think it would be nice if you let Miss Feydhev clean up before you send her out into the world? Some kind lady in Waterford must have a dress and a pair of stockings she would lend."

And then, hours and hours later, in the bright sunlight of the late afternoon, Quist lay in the king-size double bed in his apartment on Beekman Place, sleep an exhausted necessity. Lydia Morton lay beside him, holding him as if he might try to escape.

"So many of them got away," she said.

"It's tedious, routine police work," Quist said. "But sooner or later they'll have most of them. I know most of them by sight, can identify them. Kreevich will have me spending the rest of my life looking at mug shots."

Merciful sleep had almost reached him when Lydia spoke again.

"Was she pretty? Lydia asked.

"Very pretty, and more guts than you can imagine."

"Will you—do you want to see her again?"

"Yes." Quist raised up on an elbow and looked down at the woman he loved. "You'd better get some rest, too, luv," he said. "Because when I wake up I'm going to keep you very busy for a very long time."

She smiled at him. "Sleep well, darling," she said.